The Bad Mother

The Bad Mother

MARGUERITE ANDERSEN

TRANSLATION BY DONALD WINKLER

Second Story Press

Library and Archives Canada Cataloguing in Publication

Andersen, Marguerite, 1924-
[Mauvaise mère. English]
The bad mother / by Marguerite Andersen ; translated by Donald Winkler.

Translation of: La mauvaise mère.
Issued in print and electronic formats.
ISBN 978-1-927583-97-5 (paperback).—ISBN 978-1-77260-001-8 (epub)

I. Winkler, Donald, translator II. Title. III. Title: Mauvaise mère. English.

PS8551.N297M3813 2016   C843'.54   C2015-908402-4

C2015-908403-2

Originally published in French by Éditions Prise de parole, 2013 as
La mauvaise mère by Marguerite Andersen

Cover by Natalie Olsen
Cover image by designritter / photocase.com
Edited by Carolyn Jackson

Printed and bound in Canada

*Second Story Press gratefully acknowledges the support of the Ontario Arts Council
and the Canada Council for the Arts for our publishing program. We acknowledge the
financial support of the Government of Canada through the Canada Book Fund.*

ONTARIO ARTS COUNCIL
CONSEIL DES ARTS DE L'ONTARIO
an Ontario government agency
un organisme du gouvernement de l'Ontario

Canada Council   Conseil des Arts
for the Arts   du Canada

Funded by the Government of Canada
Financé par le gouvernement du Canada   Canadä

Published by
SECOND STORY PRESS
20 Maud Street, Suite 401
Toronto, ON M5V 2M5
www.secondstorypress.ca

To Jean-Jacques Rousseau,
one of the very first writers
to compose an autobiography:
his Confessions.
My text in large part follows in his footsteps...
but in the feminine.

THE BAD MOTHER

WHY

"Really, Marguerite, you're getting all worked up over nothing. Out of nowhere you're insisting that we've suffered from this — how should I put it — from this unorthodox life you led us?"

"I made you live in six different countries, on three continents. You liked that, but…"

"We saw the world."

"Yes, but let's be frank: at one point I abandoned you. I left you. And you were small."

"We survived."

"A year and a half. We were separated for a year and a half."

"That's true. But a bad mother — you?"

"Michel, let me have my say, let me tell you, let me show you. You'll see I'm right — and don't interrupt. I have to admit my mistakes, things I'm sorry for. I have to look them straight in the eye; I have to get through that narrow door. And I promise this will be the last you'll hear of it. I know… you want to believe that life's always rosy, with nuclear families, happy families, bright, healthy children, a world that's

1

close to perfect — and all the mothers are good, but—"

"Will you slow down a bit?"

"How can you believe such things when you know perfectly well that's not always the way it is?"

"What do you want me to say? Martin turned out fine — he doesn't look like he's suffering. Our sister neither, nor me, for that matter. We're not blaming you for anything."

"There's that, at least."

"We respect you."

"I know. But I blame myself for my mistakes."

"Everyone does that."

"No doubt. But a mother's mistakes— At a certain point, I deserted you, Michel."

"Listen, Mama…at your age—"

"Exactly. Before I close my eyes for good, I have to—"

"Have to what? Torment yourself?"

"Have to take stock, honestly, with no beating around the bush."

"What for?"

"To make everything a little clearer."

"Listen, you didn't torture us!"

"Just neglected you, bossed you around, sometimes ignored you — Martin especially."

"Why?"

"He was more difficult—"

"Than me? Really?"

"Yes. But never mind."

"What are you trying to say, exactly?"

"It all began with Martin. He was conceived in 1945, a glorious spring, Hitler was dead, the war was over, the whole world was exploding with joy, freedom was knocking at the door."

"Here we go, always the same old stories…"

"This time I'm not going to get bogged down in historical details. It's all about feelings, hard to define, about facts reduced to their simplest expression. And always the most pertinent. As if making notes. Poetry and prose, with or without punctuation—"

"So…a stylistic exercise?"

"Not at all!"

"A new form of self-torture?"

"Not that either."

"What then?"

"More like a quest. Like all my books. Like many books."

"A quest for transparency?[1]"

"Gropings…words that escape me…words unsaid—"

"You're still not sure?"

"Listen, my son, I thank you, but run along home now. I need to get down to work. Alone!"

---

[1] An expression originating with Jean Starobinski, who, in his *Jean-Jacques Rousseau, Transparency and Obstruction* (1957), follows, step by step, the quest for transparency, for clarity, undertaken by Rousseau.

I've always promised myself not to die
without having accomplished what I've always advised
others to effect for themselves:
an honest scrutiny of my own nature
and a serious examination of my own life.

GEORGE SAND

DECISION TAKEN

Autumn 1943. Berlin.

I'm eight years old when Hitler takes power, when my father is stripped of his duties, and I'm fifteen when the Second World War is declared. I finish high school with plans to study French language and literature, just as the doors of the Arts faculties are being closed. Forced to do war service, I catalogue all day long the innumerable x-rays of students' lungs in a Berlin University office.

It isn't much fun.

The capital bombed

three thousand dead in two nights

November 18-19 and 22-23, 1943

fires

ruins

ashes everywhere

on the ground

in the air

in the lungs

torn bodies borne away

buried

very quickly
forgotten
I flee
resume my obligatory *Kriegsdienst*
in an Austrian village nursery.

Spring 1945. Schwarzenberg. Austria.
The war is over. The radio announces that the *Führer* is dead.
Good riddance.
Go home. Go home to Berlin.
To our house.
Three women, two children: my mother, my sister Christa
with her two little ones, me.
They say there are trains. Jam-packed with women going
back to the city. Women relating their misfortunes, unable
to stop, with weary, impatient, undernourished children
screaming at the tops of their lungs.
Toilets with doors ajar or open wide, smelling of stale urine,
vomit, cheap disinfectant.
Arm yourself with silence.
Do not allow yourself to be intruded upon.
Resign yourself to a spot in the corridor, sitting on your
suitcase.
My suitcase, my mother, my sister, my nephew, my niece.
The father in Berlin.
The house still standing.
The family. Life as it should be.
As it should be?

A commonplace that merits scrutiny.
Because nothing is any more as it should be.
Nothing is like before.
There were six million human beings exterminated,
turned into objects, assassinated, still there
before our gray faces, our lowered eyes.
Shame.
Angst, a German word brought to mind with clenched teeth.
Me, I'm a coward. I'm twenty years old and I want to live.
Without fear, without shame, without hunger or thirst.
To turn my back on suffering.
To wait.
And while waiting
speak another language
laugh
distance myself.
Live with my French lover in the pleasant apartment
provided by the military.
There will be other trains.

The French lover talks of Tunis, where he was born. To
which he will return.
Is that an invitation? North Africa, marriage, a door to
freedom?
I feel myself growing wings.

A NATURAL OBSTACLE

October. No period. Not a single drop of blood.
Nausea. I start going to bed early. Sore breasts. I must be
pregnant.
Pregnant? Am I pregnant? Just like that, all of a sudden?
Naked, in front of the big bedroom mirror, I study myself.
From the front, from the side. The belly, slightly flabby.
Still the same? Yes? No! My life is changed. I am changed.
Weighed down with a belly that seems to hang heavy.
Yesterday's dream of flying, what has it become?
I am no longer she who is on the go. I am part of a we that
is going… Going where, to do what?
A child… Is that what I want? The man, the lover, does he
want that?
Have we even talked about it?
Am I really pregnant?
A child. Shouldn't I be happy?
Eager to greet it? To see it? To touch it?
A name… An image… Erika… A distant cousin.
A family secret. She had *got rid of* a child.

With the help of a doctor. Had wept afterwards, on a beach by the Baltic Sea. The child buried… Tears in the sand…
An unwanted child, accidental, a child of chance.
Unexpected.
A doctor, I need a doctor, I have to know. Let him tell me if I'm really pregnant.
"There is no doubt, Madame."
Am I not too young to be addressed like that?
I'm waiting for him to advise me, that man in white. To see the question in my eyes.
Finally he tells me that one could proceed with an abortion, yes, perhaps, given the difficult times…
But as it's illegal, the curettage would be without anaesthetic…
"You understand, if there were ever a complication… There would then be severe pain."
"Tell me, doctor, would you do that to your wife?"
My question takes him aback.
"Ah no, never, never, never!"
I'm afraid of the knife in my flesh. Mine, not that of the child.
I stand up. I put my panties back on. My shoes.
So be it, the child of chance will become my child.
I'll muddle through.

MARRIAGE

It's January and the sea is rough.

The boat pitches, everything's spinning around me, I vomit, to the right, to the left, in my bunk, on my clothes, in the toilet, overboard, I throw up what's in my stomach, all of it, to the last drop, and start all over again. Is it because I'm pregnant or because I'm seasick, or because I'm afraid of what I'm doing? Never mind, I'll never forget this wretched winter crossing of the gray Mediterranean. Shouldn't it have been blue, this sea? And me, happy?

The city.

Tunis.

Why is the air so still, so gray?

What's happened to the sun?

My lover has the banns published by the municipality's registry office. For everyone to see. Custom demands it. The law. People have ten days to object. People? Who would have a reason, any word to say, any counsel to provide? No one. I'm an unknown in the unknown, I'll say yes, I'll sign a document, bear another name.

My lover has also changed. He's no longer the proud

conqueror, the joyous liberator of my country, he's once
more become the bureaucrat of his pre-war past.

Must I marry him?

Climbing the few steps leading to the city hall door, I see my
mistake.

Marry?

Share my life, day and night, with another?

For a child?

Protest, Marguerite, cry *stop*, declare that you're not going
to marry! Not today, not with him, pregnant as you are, no,
you don't want to get married… You're strong, you'll make
out on your own… Tell the man and his two witnesses that
you have to turn back, go for a drink somewhere, there, in
this bar, at the corner, talk things through calmly. Chew on a
few sunflower seeds…

I cross the threshold.

Have I the right to deprive this child of its father?

Is that a sentimental question?

Who will give me an answer?

The child can't express itself.

Who understands the language of punches or kicks against
uterus walls?

For a few seconds

far from my family

from those I really know

alone

pregnant

forced by my nature and my actions to harbor a child in the
making

I am confused.

What would the civil servant do with an hour come

suddenly free, there in his humdrum office where his

secretary will perhaps set down a bouquet of blue, white, red

anemones to brighten the ceremony?

And me, what would I do?

The sea, Europe, Berlin…

I'm lightheaded

I don't know which way to turn.

I'd like to proclaim aloud that the banns must be cancelled,

erased, forgotten,

that I'm not the merry fiancée, the woman one should

marry,

the mother ready to raise a child.

I'd like to sit down, there,

on that gray bench

in the corridor

and let spill all my body's tears.

Am I wrong, am I right?

Who will tell me?

Words swim round in my head:

Affentheater, foolery, nonsense…

I step into the office where the marriage will take place.

In my sightline, the exit, opening onto a difficult life.

CUPPING GLASSES AND HORSE BLOOD

Her name is Clémentine. A Corsican, a black-clad widow, small, proud, a post office employee, thin-skinned and energetic.

Old, it seems to me.

Her son Jean and I, the pregnant daughter-in-law, are staying with her

in her apartment at 43, rue de Bretagne, which is tiny, cramped, filled with worn, varnished furniture.

In the morning, Clémentine hands me a glass of horse blood, good for the mother-to-be, and offers, as soon as I cough — but so little, that rainy spring — to bleed me with cupping glasses. So as not to cross her, I go along with it. She, on the other hand, mocks my yearning for hot baths. "Marguerite, really, you've been bred to luxury and extravagance!"

I don't like being treated like a spoiled daughter.

My parents were never *rich*.

I withdraw a little. Try not to take up too much space. Smile politely. Stay silent.

I'm silent when the old woman comes back from the market
with a live chicken, its legs bound together, when she
prepares to cut the throat of the visibly nervous bird, asks
me to hold the dish sprinkled with finely chopped onions to
catch the blood:
"That will fry up well!"
I remain silent too when the mother and son burst into
laughter at the sight of the decapitated fowl lurching about
in the narrow kitchen.
"Catch it, catch it!" the son cries to me.
I stop smiling.
No! I'm not at a loss for words.
I'm afraid of letting loose with what I'd like to say.
Cut off by the sea from what is familiar,
I fear an unknown future
the man on whom my day-to-day life
now depends
the old woman who he says
can be furious "when something comes over her."
Something, is what?
The child will be born into my unease.

PUSH, MADAME!

June, 1946. I'm stretched out on a gynaecological table
in the birth room of the clinic named for Saint Augustine,
he who thought women to be forever blessed.
Around me, all in white:
the walls
the ceilings
the doors
the window frames, their curtains
the beds and sheets
the habits of the good sisters
nurses and midwives
everything gleams white
while stainless steel instruments tinkle away.
I am cold.
The midwife holds my hand, the obstetrician
sits on a stool between my legs
lashed into stirrups.
I am parturient.
"Push, Madame," says the midwife, "push!"
What am I supposed to push?

No one has explained to me the mechanics of labor.
Contraction, dilation, expulsion, delivery…
I know nothing.
"Push, push!"
I want to sleep.
But already the child is slipping out of me, I hear its cry.
They cut the cord, weigh the newborn, wipe away all sorts
of viscous liquids, wrap it up, put it into my arms and
inform me that it's a boy, take it away from me, deposit it
in a little white crib. Poor thing. Is it dizzied by all these
manipulations?
"Everything is fine, Madame," says the doctor, before going
on his way.
Here I am alone, in a room, in a bed. I feel light, there's
no longer another person in my belly. Nine months have
passed. My body is again all mine.
But, alone?
No.
Beside my bed, there's a smaller bed, a baby, a child, my
child, my son.
I raise myself up, bend gently over the nearby crib, look at
the little man who has come out of me.
Is that it, to have a child?
A black shock of hair. Face a bit red. He's resting.
Breathing. Sleeping. What is he dreaming?
Can he already dream?
I touch his fingers.
He pays no attention.

I was fourteen years old when Christa had her first child. I saw her take care of it, I'll learn to take care of mine. For a while. A few years. Twenty?

For a long time, that's clear.

There's no doubt, Madame.

Here I am, a mother. Definitively. Irrevocably a mother for life.

Overcome by a kind of mildness I've never before experienced.

And I'm afraid to touch him.

Fear and desire. Fear of hurting him, desire to know him.

In any case, I'm in no hurry. We have time. Him and me. We'll live together.

I turn my head towards the window.

Lanes, ponds, lawns. The Belvedere park. Pines, low palms, tall palms, eucalyptus, flowers everywhere, big clumps of scarlet bougainvillea and pink laurels. Hills in the distance. The sky still blue. Let the night arrive with its stars...

To sleep.

I don't know what awaits me: A hard life in a language that is not yet mine, in a colonial milieu, in a land noted for its dazzling white architecture accented by the blue of its studded doors and its wrought iron mashrabiyas the color of the sky. A land that for lack of time and money I will not explore, no, I must busy myself with the child, the cleaning, the laundry, the wet clothes hung out on the terrace under a sky always so blue, taking pleasure in a short moment with a view of the white city, going quickly back down, rushing to the central market while the little one's sleeping, admiring the wealth of fruits and vegetables, buying the least expensive, hurrying home with a full basket, preparing and serving lunch for the man back from the office, doing the dishes, changing diapers, putting the child to sleep, having a nap with the husband, taking in the laundry, ironing the man's shirts, two a day, with small irons heated on the stove, changing diapers again and always again, taking the child for a walk in its pram, pushing it along the avenue Jules-Ferry, which will become the avenue Habib-Bourguiba on the day of liberation, up to the wonderful open space reserved for florists — nobody buys me flowers — then back without dawdling to prepare and serve the dinner, wash the dishes, put them away, put the child to bed, go to sleep exhausted after having made love, often without wanting to, to get up in the morning full of energy, yes, but dismayed by the multitude of daily tasks.

In short, obliged to organize my time to conform with that of others, of my family, according to the conventions laid down by society.

In a five hour morning she makes breakfast for the children, washes them, dresses them, cleans the house, makes the beds, washes herself, dresses, does errands, cooks, sets the table, feeds the children for twenty minutes, shouts at them, takes them to school, does the dishes, does the washing and the rest, and the rest. Perhaps, around three-thirty, she might, for half an hour, read a newspaper.

MARGUERITE DURAS

INTERLUDE

After the birth, Corsican cousins about to leave for a
summer on the island, offer us their apartment.
Dark and chaotic, with no real color, crammed full of
furniture, mirrored wardrobes, sideboards, voluminous
padded armchairs, rugs, heavy curtains, baubles without
end.
I find it hard to breathe.
As soon as the lights go off, Martin asserts himself. He cries,
wails, as only babies can. Gentle words, caresses, a bottle
with slightly sweetened water…nothing works.
He's afraid, I tell myself, it's his first night out in the world.
His father suggests tossing him out of the window.
A real threat or an awkward joke?
Instinctively, the thirty-three vertebrae of my spinal column
stiffen, a surge of energy puts my shoulders on the alert.
I'm the mother protecting her child.
I push the cradle into another room, sit by its side, leave a
light on, and rock my son, hoping to erase all malice from
his memory.

And then I see them: an entire army of tiny insects crawling along the sheets, towards his pink skin…

I catch them, crush them.

In the morning, his father laughs.

"Bed bugs," he says.

I panic, demand explanations, an instant remedy. He has to do something, for heaven's sake. He shrugs his shoulders, goes to work.

How to get rid of bugs that suck the blood of a newborn?

Is it stress? A few days of this and I'm sick.

We call the doctor, who finds a practical solution:

"Two weeks' rest in the clinic, mother and child! Meanwhile, sir, try to find an apartment that's free of vermin!"

Back with the smiling sisters, in beds without bugs, at peace, in a bright room with no superfluous furnishings and doodads.

RECLUSE

A high-rise at the end of avenue Jules-Ferry. From the kitchen window, by craning my neck, I can make out a tiny slice of the Mediterranean.

I turn towards the inside. I observe my son. I'm gentle with him. It's very natural, perfectly natural, it goes without saying, it's to be assumed.

They say that maternal love begins when the milk comes....

Yet I bottle-feed Martin...

Powdered Nestlé buttermilk mixed with boiled water, as the pediatrician prescribes. As the instructions on the yellow tin suggest.

My milk doesn't come.

I do not give my breast to my child.

Was I advised to do so? Was I advised not to?

Am I afraid of such intimacy?

Breast feeding is not in fashion.

No one has even mentioned it to me.

Does he miss my breast?

Is he not satisfied?

Almost every day, I note the progress he makes: look, he's smiling, listen to him gurgle; look, he's sucking his thumb; look, you'd think he was following me with his eyes, I give him the rattle, he takes it and shakes it, he's fascinated by his hands, he imitates the sounds I make, turns around; look, he wants to sit up; there's his first tooth already, that's why he was crying so much yesterday.

There's no softer skin than his.

I sing him the song about hands that *do this, this, this…*

Look, he's laughing, he's crawling, look, he's trying to stand up, he's walking and holding on…

He seems perfect to me.

Day and night
we're together
the indoors is our world
we belong to one another.

Only the child matters to me.

Is that it, mother love?

LOVE

And the other love? The great love described by the poets?
That I should feel for my husband, the man of my life?
Nothing like that in me, today. Nor yesterday.
But we gave ourselves pleasure once, did we not?
Love has become a deed to accomplish at the end of the
evening, to finish the day, to bring on the night.
A dessert foretold in advance, writes Flaubert, *after the*
monotony of dinner.
A routine that goes stale.
Frozen ground.
Is my son cold, as well?
In this apartment near the port, the man leans over me,
kisses me. Does he not feel that I remain almost motionless?
No, he continues to draw near me, I don't want to say to
him that, alas, this leaves me indifferent. I don't want to
wound him, to provoke his contempt, his disgust, his bad
humor.
The man penetrates me at last, without my really reacting.
Boredom envelops me.

Every evening I dread the night, and the man who believes he has the right to take hold of me when his body urges him to do so. I only want to sleep. Not to be disturbed. To drop into sleep, a sleep that's inert, dreamless even, if that were only possible.

One morning when it's still gray, a lost rat enters by the French window, open wide, leaps onto the bed, crosses over it. It realizes its mistake, and quickly flees.

The port is not far off.

The port. Boats. Liners.

Two secret passengers in the hold of a ship?

A mother and her child?

A mad idea.

I would have liked that.

I couldn't save us.

I lacked the courage.

THE BOLT

One day, when the tenant below hears me bringing the pram
down one step after another, *boom, boom, boom,* and again
boom, he comes out to help me.
"Schmitz, my name is Eric Schmitz, I'm an old German Jew,
happy to talk to you in his mother tongue."
We exchange memories. Berlin, his city, my city, the
Kurfürstendamm, the Grunewald, the rivers and lakes,
the zoo, the double-level buses, the subway, the cafés, the
theaters, the museums…
So there we are, I have a friend, we smile at each other,
Guten Tag and *Grüss Gott*, step in for a minute… I sip a
coffee or a glass of wine, savor a Danish pastry, get news
about Germany from my host, who's an avid reader of the
papers. He offers me books, magazines, *alles auf Deutsch*. Do
come in, why yes, the little one too of course, he's cute, I'll
offer you a drink, you have plenty of time…
I forget the clock, until suddenly I exclaim: *Ach du liebe
Güte, mein Mann!* He must be home… I have to run…
I laugh, I don't want to leave, this gentleman's apartment
reminds me of my father's office, there are books everywhere,

old engravings on the walls, dictionaries…
I run, I've totally forgotten the tomato sauce on the stove…

The innocent friendship between a friendly old man and a
solitary young woman will end with an injunction:
"I don't want you seeing Monsieur Schmitz."
Speechless before this assault on my freedom, I do not voice
my anger. I'm like the young horse kicking over the traces,
except the young horse would make his voice heard, would
rear up, would try to strike out with his hooves, while I
remain still, and silent.
Because there's a threat. The day I came back late , my
husband had waited for me. Furious. He'd clearly seen the
carriage on the landing, in front of Monsieur Schmitz's
door, he could have rung, but he went up to the apartment,
turned off the burner under the tomatoes, sat down.
"And so," he'd grumbled, "we're having fun with the
neighbor? The Kraut? Does he kiss well, the dirty Yid?"
I'd laughed outright at such brutality, burst into tears, cried
that I couldn't take it any more, that I wanted to go home to
my parents, my country, my city…
In his role as police inspector
the man then warned me
smiling wickedly
that all the border posts would as of the next day be advised
to stop me, a young woman with or without a baby,
passport, ticket, it didn't matter!

"You won't get through!"

I was frozen with fear.

The Nazis had taught me to beware of those whose role it was to enforce the law. I'd never forgotten that lesson.

I could have cried for help. But who would have heard me?

The bolt had been thrown, and the spouse, me, thwarted.

THERE IS STILL ROOM AT THE INN

Martha, my very good mother, senses the melancholy behind my letters' ramblings: *Everyone's fine... Martin now has more than ten teeth... He loves the flower displays at the end of the wide avenue... I always want to buy some, but that wouldn't be sensible... It's the season for peas... I bought a kilo and a half at the market, I'll need time to shell them...*
She's just moved her husband and daughter Christa to London.
What luck, those British passports, Theo's birth in Ghana, on English soil, where his father was a missionary... It's Eve, the oldest daughter, who, married to a Jewish businessman, had in 1933 learned of that opening, enabling them to leave Germany.
Theo teaches in the denazification program for German prisoners of war. Christa works as a barmaid, her children are enrolled in the neighborhood school; she's waiting for her husband, one of the prisoners Theo is teaching, to be discharged. Martha is running a bed and breakfast in Hampstead Heath, a neighborhood where Eve and John
— she's exchanged her businessman for a Canadian — and

their son live. Why should Marguerite and Martin not join the group? There's still room at the inn.

Come, your ticket's waiting at the Air France office.

And I fly away.

Nothing could hold me. Not vain threats, nor big promises.

Martin in my arms, I arrive in London.

"Don't think of anything," says Martha, "don't explain anything. You're tired. Go up to your room, you'll see, the one with the yellow curtains. Leave the little one, I'll take care of him."

Ah! To be able to close a door behind me, with no worries. To sleep.

"Martin," she says the next day, "has lacked for nothing, he had a snooze also."

"About six o'clock," adds Theo, "I went out with him. We walked around by the light of the street lamps, prettily cloaked in a light fog. I recited him a bit of Saint-Exupéry…"

It is the peaceful life of the clan. If the family is not rich, it comports itself with grace.

In the evening, there's a gathering.

People discuss a thousand things: politics, literature, art, anything goes. Germany. Its loss.

Its reconstruction.

I listen, I absorb. Hungrily.

In Tunis, people talked to me of nothing, and I talked to no one.

I won't go back.

I write a letter.

Two weeks later, the man arrives. Rings the doorbell. I don't answer.

"We can't leave him in the street," says the wise Christa.

How will this visit end?

Every day, he tries to persuade me.

"You like Tunis a lot."

"Yes, but I'm not going back."

"And what will you live on here? It's not me who's going to send you money."

"I'll work in a restaurant, a hotel."

I'll teach French, I'll do translation.

The arguments repeat themselves.

Discreet, the family members don't intervene.

At mealtime, Theo shows off his knowledge of French.

"Tunisia is a French protectorate," he remembers, "is that a good thing?"

The answer remains vague. Justifying colonialism is not what's on the visitor's mind.

Martha, always pleasant, knows how to keep her distance.

Would I be able to go back and live with him?

Be his, as they say?

No!

He tries to show concern for my parents.

"Your mother is tired of being a servant to her tenants."

"It's her choice. And it's probably temporary. One day, they'll go back to Germany."

"And you?"

"We'll see."

"And my son?"

"I'll make out."

"I only have five more days. October 20…"

I know, everyone knows. The return date is set.

The day before the stranger's departure there occurs what is called an act of love.

What was I thinking?

Did I pity him?

Did I say to myself that once wouldn't hurt?

Pointless questions.

A fetus is lodged in my uterus, resists all attempts at abortion, jumping over and over from table to floor, a parsley infusion, quinine…

Nothing.

Not a drop of blood.

Nausea.

I'm desperate.

I'm ashamed.

Theo talks of returning to Berlin. The rebirth of democracy.

Christa, her husband, and their children are ready to go back to Germany.

Eve and her husband are thinking of leaving England to settle in Montreal

like so many others.

And me?

I stumble around

I don't know what to do

me

with no trade, no professional training

to throw myself into an independent life?

Impose two children on my parents?
Attach myself to Eve along with them?
Wie man sich bettet, so liegt man
you've made your bed, lie in it
my two languages repeat to me
I repeat to myself
I'll have two children to hold by the hand,
two children of chance,
born of the carelessness for which I blame myself
today still.
Both hands taken up
with a thousand large and small tasks to complete for them
from morning to evening
and at night as well
without stopping
in a tenuous and fragile nest, the only one I have to offer
them,
where I will try to do the best I can.
Me, the thoughtless and featherbrained mother.

THE SAME AND DIFFERENT

July 1948. The second child is born. Slowly. Very slowly.
Once again, I only want to sleep.
An episiotomy opens me up, lets the eleven-pound baby
work its way through.
"He's beautiful," the midwife exclaims.
The doctor repositions himself on the stool between my legs
puts on his glasses
threads the needle
aims it, inserts it, repairs me.
Like a housewife mending a sock.
No anaesthetic.
"There, Madame, it will hurt. Here, there are no nerves,
you'll feel nothing."
Martha, the good mother, the excellent mother, who has
come as she promised, holds me by the hand.
The big baby seems to smile.
At home, his brother acts out his confusion by knocking his
head, during the night, against the side of his bed.
His father is sleeping. I'm sleeping.

"You didn't hear him?" Martha asks in the morning, "He must be upset."

No, really, at night I shut the bedroom door, I'm aware of nothing, I've not been awakened by any distress on the part of Martin, I didn't hear him calling. I didn't rush to comfort him. In short, already two years old, Martin is a difficult child with a tired mother, herself difficult as well, deaf to her son's sorrow.

Martha takes him out in the sun. Lets him run to the beggar whom he embraces on the avenue Jules-Ferry.

She laughs:

"He has a compassionate nature. He mustn't lose it."

As for me, she gives me a warning:

"You only have one body, my dear, don't overextend yourself," she says, before leaving for Europe.

I store her advice deep in my memory.

AD INFINITUM

I continue to provide for the others, I prepare meals,
with the help of my mother-in-law I learn to make soups,
soufflés, salads, pastas with all sorts of sauces, couscous, head
cheese, tripe in the style of Caen or Lyon, and other foods
that are not too expensive, fish, a leg of lamb, perhaps, on
Sunday, when she comes to lunch. Desserts as well, crème
caramel, rice cakes, crêpes, fritters, pies, clafoutis, floating
islands, meringues.
Is there any end to all these recipes?
A good mother, I make jams: strawberry, apricot, quince.
I remember my apprenticeship in sewing and knitting at
the German school, I don't much like this sort of women's
work, but I sew clothes for my children, knit them rompers,
sweaters, and tuques.
The tile floor is always clean. Clothes washed by hand. A
washboard, a big piece of Marseille soap, each article rinsed,
wrung out and hung out on the terrace to greet the sun...
My husband's shirts
his underpants
my panties

all swirl in the water
float in the wind
dried, ironed, folded, sorted,
above all don't forget the diapers
squares of white cotton
at least a dozen a day.
Tomorrow is today's twin.
I make no headway through the ordered labyrinth of the
household work imposed on me.
Outings?
Six years of pushing in front of me carriage, stroller, carriage,
stroller
one child reclined or sitting up
the other holding my hand.
Exercises to strengthen the arms?
I'd have preferred something more varied.

IN THE SHADOW OF THE TWO-HORNED MOUNTAIN

We move to Saint-Germain[2]. The suburbs. Cheaper rent.
Within the village, a small apartment in the house of a
former railway worker.
Far off, Mount Boukornine,
today a reference for young people who sing its praises on
Facebook
its pink cyclamens, their scent, its always being there.
The volcano that sleeps
so near me
in 1950.
A garden of a few square meters, but still a garden.
A vine climbing the courtyard's walls.
Heavy muscat grapes offering free dessert.
The pomegranate tree with glossy green leaves, red flowers
male and hermaphrodite, sports fruits with skin hard as
leather, behind which hide hundreds of plump, juicy seeds
with their tart coating. A bit of red wine, a bit of sugar, and
here's another dessert.
Then the fig tree

---

[2] Today Ezzahra

broad and strong
with its branches stretched out
a tree never trimmed
loaded with green figs
in my memory still.
It's morning.
The nocturnal dogs have gone silent,
the goats have already passed through.
Nothing moves.
I listen to the silence
enjoy the sight of the large leaves
the fruits velvet to the touch
I gather one that will melt on my tongue
voluptuously.
Then there's the sea. Five hundred meters away.
Every day, the sea.
To see it, to breathe it in, to touch it, I feel welcomed.
A mild summer morning, stretched out on the blue, calm
water,
I float on my back.
I float.
Will the Mediterranean bear me away? The temptation to let
myself go is strong. Arms extended, eyes open to the sky, so
blue as well, I drift into a vacant dream.
"Mama!"
Martin needs his mother.
Really?
In any case, the dream is over.
I rush back to the beach and day-to-day reality.

CHALLENGES

Two rooms: the entrance, two meters by four, will serve as
a dining room. On the left is the children's room, with a
window giving onto the garden. On the right is the married
couple's bedroom, with its oil-painted walls, dark gray, a
railroad color. A border of large yellow lemons separates the
walls from the ceiling.
Do you know the land where lemon trees flower?
asks Goethe
the elegant traveler with his wide-brimmed hat,
his gaze fixed on the distant Roman countryside
a work of Tischbein
a famous canvas, near to gigantic
from another time.
Too big for our apartments, said the poet
and the portrait has nothing to do with the railroad worker's
apartment
except for the lemons
poorly painted
asserting at the top of the wall
that this is the much-coveted South.

Then
in no time at all
without warning
there suddenly reappears
the oh-so potent banality of the real:
a bathroom with no shower or tub, a washbasin
with cold running water, a WC,
a cramped kitchen outside.
To reach it you must exit the apartment
walk down two steps
cross the courtyard while skirting everything that's in the
way:
tricycles, toys, cacti, basins, brooms, shoes and bric-a-brac,
climb two steps to the kitchen door,
open it and at last gain access to this important space
where there's a cold water tap over a sink.
Weighed down with food, plates and utensils, I go
constantly back and forth,
more or less groping my way.
Such challenges don't daunt me: the Austrian farm, the
family refuge during the fearful war, had no running water,
we found it outside where a spring, natural but tamed,
flowed bright and melodious into a hollowed-out tree
stump.
No bathroom, no WC, just a *Plumpsko*, a kind of shed
with a hole in a board, a trench into which things fell with
resonance and energy.
No electricity? At night we lit one or two oil lamps. The
wood stove stood in for the electric range in Berlin.

At Schwarzenberg, Martha spared no effort making life agreeable for all.

At Saint-Germain, I tried to do the same. No gas? I'd try to cook on a Primus, like so many Tunisian women.

Oh, how I hate the Primus!
I despise the Primus
fine for camping
awful for everyday
family meals.
I'd like to toss it in the garbage
this object that bit by bit comes to personify
my unhappy marriage.
I'd like to blow it up
kick it to death
pound it with a hammer or a jackhammer,
with a monkey wrench or a mallet,
oh, give me a chain saw that will slice through metal!
But every day
instead of setting it on fire, in my fury
I polish the monster.
The family wants its meals
its countless meals
two hot meals per day

seven hundred and thirty each year
for how many years to come?
I like to see them eat
my children
but I abhor
this instrument devised by a Swede in 1892
a daily ordeal
whose routine is always the same.
I make sure the reservoir's filled with kerosene.
The smell is strong.
My hands reek.
I pour a bit of this liquid into the pan under the burner,
strike a match, start the fire.
I wait a minute for the burner to heat up.
I take hold of the little pump.
One would think it an act of love,
but I'm just cooking a meal.
Careful! To stop the flames, the soot, and that horrible odor
from seeping into what I'm preparing, I have to keep the
pots well sealed...
But I'm shrewd. I do it deliberately, I decide that from
time to time there'll be a conspicuous taste of petrol. Those
"accidents" lead to the purchase of a butane burner.

Here I am, delighted with my Butagaz.... Who would have
believed it?

THE CESSPOOL

Whatever the century in the history of the world,
I see the woman
in a restricted, untenable situation,
dancing on a wire looking down on death
MARGUERITE DURAS

The most arduous challenge is the cesspool. A simple hole
in the garden, made watertight with bricks and stones, and
topped with a heavy cement slab two meters square. There
is poured the dirty water: cleaning water, water from the
kitchen, the bathroom, the WC.
This pit, whose depth I haven't measured, fills up quickly.
Every month it has to be emptied.
There's a worker, Ali, prepared to do it, but we're short of
money. To the point where sometimes I don't know if I can
risk buying a half-pound of ground meat to mix with the
tomato sauce, or if I have to ask the friendly grocer from
Djerba to give me credit. So how to pay Ali?
I don't have the means.
And so the housewife takes care of the sewage.

With an iron bar I shift the slab, plunge a pail attached to a
broomstick into the black liquid, repugnant, where fat white
bugs are swimming.
I lift it out and pour its contents into a hole already
dug in another corner of the garden. Strewn with these
supplementary cesspools into which I'm afraid they'll slip,
the garden is out of bounds for my sons, as is the little
kitchen where they risk overturning the Primus crowned
with a couscous-maker or a pot of boiling water for
spaghetti.
I don't overprotect my sons.
I let them run in the street
cavort after the rains in the muddy field between us
and Mount Boukornine,
but from that to courting real danger…
When I think…
How can you keep two tireless little mischief-makers clean?

THE NIGHTLY BATHS

The big pot of hot water
brought from the outside kitchen to the bathroom inside
poured into the cold water that already fills a good part of
the little tin tub just big enough to hold two children ready
to be washed...
I like to see them
first covered in suds
then all clean
hair flattened by the water
the little pecker under the bulging belly
tanned skin
feet so soft...
hands that slap the water
the water splashes
we laugh
quickly
dry the body
rub the back
the hair
I love them

with passion and pleasure.
Then I become mother Hercules
one-two-three
I lift the tub
pour the water into the toilet
from where it will flow to fill the pit
that, alas, will then have to be emptied.
A vicious circle I'll have to repeat without telling the
children that what they find fun is hard, that I'm sometimes
fed up, that sometimes I laugh only to laugh with them.

VIOLENCE

On Martin's first day at school, he starts to cry. Sitting under and not at his desk, he tells the teacher he much prefers his mother to her and in the following weeks he takes a long time learning the alphabet, which seems to him perfectly useless, as do numbers. He's happy counting to five, since he's five years old, but prefers to stop there.

Six like sausage, seven like sucker, knowing my son's tastes, I sing the numbers to him.

He pays no attention.

I laugh it off. I like it when my sons revolt.

There are about twenty-three pupils in the kindergarten, and only one, him, resists what seems normal to the others.

Is he stupid? No one says it, but that's what they think. Is he too spoiled? His affection for his mother is touching. The least one can say is that he's not easy.

The father takes off his belt to beat this son who doesn't want to recite his numbers, declares in a loud, nasty voice that he'll now be getting his *well-deserved thrashing*.

That there will be more to come if he keeps on refusing to learn by heart what's being thrust on him.

"Drop your pants!"

My son trembles. Looks at me anxiously.

"Drop your underwear!"

The blows on his innocent, white little behind.

No one ever beat me, and yet I don't intervene.

Would a good mother not have protected her son?

Am I afraid for myself?

Would a good mother not have known how to make her son understand that school is a useful and necessary thing?

Am I a good enough mother when, the blows and cries having stopped, I take the child in my arms? When I wipe his sorrowful tears from his cheek? And gently caress his bruised bottom?

Or am I simply a coward?

"Mama!"

Seize the belt, throw yourself into the fray, scream

"Stop!"

at the violent man.

Defend your child.

In 2013, I read Elie Wiesel, who at Buchenwald had not dared defend his father against an officer's blows:

An officer passed between the bunks. My father was pleading: "My son, water... I'm burning up... My insides..." "Silence over there!" barked the officer.

"Eliezer," continued my father, "water…"
The officer came closer and shouted to him to be silent. But
my father did not hear. He continued to call me. The officer
wielded his club and dealt him a violent blow to the head.
I didn't move. I was afraid, my body was afraid of another
blow, this time to my head.

                                    NIGHT (Hill & Wang, 2006)

In the preface to this edition, Wiesel recalled:

I shall never forgive myself.
(…)
His last word had been my name. A summons. And I had not
responded.

I'm ashamed to associate my inaction with the misfortune of
Elie Wiesel, whose words are riveting.
My child didn't die. There was no SS in the house at Saint-
Germain, just a brutal man and my son, appealing to me.

In time, he ends up learning his numbers and letters, his
father no longer beats him, but I, the mother of that child,
still do not comprehend how I did not protest against that
violent act.
Terrified, deprived of maternal protection, half naked, my
son was in the process of losing his sense of security. His
body knew that it was in danger, that he was small, that his

father was bigger and stronger than him.

His only support, his mother, big and strong as well, having abandoned him, he could not flee.

And I, how could I serve this man his food, sit beside him, eat, and perhaps let him make love to me at night, with the beaten child in the next room?

I disgust myself, I make myself small.

Today, old, I try to understand.

I DON'T SEEK, I FIND[3]

Does he sense my quiet desperation? Without saying
anything, Theo, my father, sends me French books from
his collection: Pascal, Voltaire, Rousseau, Balzac, Stendhal,
Flaubert, Zola, Baudelaire, Proust.
The list is long and I am hungry.
I feed myself on books.
I read while waiting for the couscous to be ready, the
potatoes to be cooked, the soufflé done.
Let the children and husband sleep.
I read, I improve myself.
Coincidence?
Suddenly, I realize that I have a gift: did I not take care
of my sister's children, and those in the Austrian village
nursery?
My experience becomes marketable.
The entrance-dining room, three times a week, is
transformed into a kindergarten where one paints pictures,
sings and dances, and where I earn a modest amount of
pocket money by supervising four children

---

[3] Picasso

51

whose mothers work outside the home…
That I could do the same has not yet entered my mind.

DOORS OPEN

In 1953, Michel, the levelheaded
mute witness
to the blows from a belt that Martin received
joins his brother at the village school.
They go there on foot
talking along the way
happy
to be together.
To a degree, I am now free.
I seek and find a teaching job, learn to drive my husband's
old Peugeot, start to enjoy my freedom, making the twenty
kilometer trip to a high school three times a week to teach
young North Africans who'd rather be playing football,
everything that's wanted.
The principal asks:
"You're of German origin, Madame? Then you ought to be
able to give them an appreciation of classical music."
"You're European? You'll introduce them to ancient Greece."
"And then geography? This year, it will be winds and
currents."

"And English, if you like."

I don't know much about geography, nothing about winds and currents. But what would I not do to earn the meager salary I'm offered, and to pass through the doors opening up for me? Every night, when the children are put to bed, I prepare the classes for the next day.

One difficulty to overcome: I don't have the French nationality required to be able to teach in Tunisia, a French protectorate. Married to a Frenchman, I obtain my naturalization.

Here I am with three nationalities, proud of being a citizen of the world…

Me, a modest homebody, where am I going to travel?

And when? I dare not think about it.

But the same year, I enroll in a literature course at the *Institut des Hautes Études* in Tunis.

I'm thirty years old, and I'm so thirsty.

Thirsty for knowledge, thirsty for the outside world, thirsty for freedom, thirsty for pleasure as well.

Thirst, thirst, thirst!

UP THE ROCKFACE

The unconscious does not think or calculate.
In a sense, it does not judge.
It is happy just to transform.

FREUD

Saturday afternoon, it's volleyball with the neighbors.
What did they think of this poorly-matched couple?
No memory. Only that of the pleasure of the moment.
Sunday afternoon, it's bridge. Five or six hours of leisure per
week.
And the children?
I am distancing myself from my children.
During the day they're at school, I don't see them, don't
hear them, don't touch them for hours. Of course, I don't
forget them, naturally we're together, but my concentration
on them wavers, no longer hovers over them; the constant
surveillance is no more.
I have time to learn,
to entertain doubts regarding the little I know.
Nothing will stop me.
The bad mother is asserting herself.

FORBIDDEN TERRITORY, AGAIN

"Marguerite, it's for tomorrow, Zaghwan. We leave at eight-thirty, we'll be back by three o'clock. Seventy kilometers, it's nothing. And the aqueduct has to be seen!"
For weeks, Claude, who plays bridge and volleyball with us, has been talking about showing me Tunisia beyond Tunis, outside of Saint-Germain. A representative of Shell Tunis, he travels frequently around the countryside.
"I'll be ready."
I spend the evening dreaming about this excursion, imagining the ruins of the aqueduct between Zaghwan and Carthage that provided second century Carthaginians with drinking water.
The children will be at school, I have no courses to give or to take.
Happiness! I'll see the country…
To see…
In the morning, Jean's face is shut down, sign of a bad day.
"I don't want you going off with Claude. Let him take his own wife if he wants company. I forbid it… I won't let you…"

Silent, I watch him leave.

I'm standing outside the garden's metal gate, painted blue,
like all Tunisian gates.

Ah! How much I love the color blue

the blue of mashrabiyas against the white walls

the blue of my eldest son's eyes…

I'm waiting for Claude in his Renault 4:

"He doesn't want me to…"

"And?"

"We'll see…"

"You're sure?"

"Yes."

Claude turns on the radio. *Padam, padam*, sings Edith Piaf.

"Watch carefully, Marguerite, let me know when you see the
first arch."

I watch.

Olive trees, fields, a man in a red fez on his donkey, children
running barefoot

palm trees with long leaves dancing in the wind

rows of gray-green olive trees…

What did Baudelaire say?

Enivrez-vous! Exult!

First stop at Mohammedia

Ruins of a bey's palace.

A coffee before moving on.

Two minutes and I'm crying out:

"There!"

One, no three, no seven stone arches, high, solid even in
their ruin, and it goes on,

it's as if the aqueduct were playing hide-and-seek with us. When you think it's finished, it starts all over again…

Beautiful images inscribe themselves in my memory.

Claude recites:

"A hydrological system, a hundred and thirty-two kilometers, bricks and blocks of sandstone, at ground level and up above, buried and airborne, drinking water, three hundred and seventy liters per second…"

"How do you know all that, Claude?"

"Oh, reading, visiting museums… We'll stop here…"

"We're…"

"At Oudna, once called Uthina, where a young Dreyfusard archeologist…"

"…Dreyfusard?"

"Really, Marguerite!"

"I'm ignorant, Claude, a German woman who knows nothing…"

"Nonsense! Anyway, the Dreyfus affair was a societal conflict at the end of the nineteenth century. The archeologist discovered at Oudna a big house full of mosaics, had them transported to the museum at Bardo.

It's beautiful, you should go there."

We arrive at Zaghwan.

A temple of waters or a nymphaeum, a basin shaped like an eight in front of a colonnade of twelve niches, behind which is a wood where I, the undisciplined disciple, linger to pick raspberries.

Finally I say, "I'm tired."

"Okay. I just need half an hour to talk to a colleague. Go to the village, there's a market today, I'll find you there, we'll eat and go back…"

An eventful day, with eyes wide open.

An initiation into the world of knowledge, without my even knowing.

THE BATTERED WOMAN

The children come home from school.
The man comes home from work.
We eat dinner in silence.
The children sense a conflict, go to bed without complaint.
For them, bed is a refuge.
Silence.
More silence.
Then violence.
Blows.
Insults.
"Bitch! Whore! Fucking Kraut!"
Say nothing. Don't cry. Don't moan. Don't wake the
children.
Shame. Shame at being so weak, so cowardly, of being a
battered woman.
Run away? But where? To say…
"He beat me…"
To say it to whom?
"What's that, mama? That blue mark on your face?"

"I bumped into something, don't worry, my love. It's nothing serious."

Weak. Cowardly.

Helpless to act.

To tell the neighbors why all diversions are forbidden.

To kill.

To take the gun.

To see blood,

go to prison.

No.

Endure the blows, the wounds, the insults.

Say nothing. Obey.

Sleep in the same bed, there is no other.

Shame. Disgust. Stifled rage. Impossible to put it out of mind.

Acts pictured.

Words in the head.

Words with no breath to speak them.

THE AGE OF REASON

I pull myself together.
I take myself in hand.
I don't want to live unhappy.
I go to bed early so as to be in form the next day,
get up early, wake the children,
they go to school, happy, lacking for nothing.
I am the good mother.
I run off to teach, to study,
I'll be back home when, happy, they return.
I laugh with them
at their pranks
at their silliness
at what they tell me.
On the fly,
a snack of fruits, of dates perhaps, of biscuits.
They go out to play with the neighborhood children
and come home for dinner.
I am the nurturing mother,
I kiss them, they go to sleep happy.
I, ambitious, hungry,

I read, I write, I soak up knowledge.

During those hours, curiously, I am left in peace.

Has his French education instilled in this man a respect for intellectual pursuits? Does he imagine that one of these days I'll earn a lot of money?

That is not what I'm after.

EMPTINESS

June 1954.
Exams passed. Summer vacation. The beach. The sea.
I lie out in the sun, my body relaxes.
My sons run around with the other children, move off,
come back.
I hear their voices, I reply, they run off again.
I just have to be there
present
available
at every moment.
But there's a void somewhere.
My children, the sun, the sea, and a hundred little things,
I like them,
but somewhere
very near
there is this void
that burns, hurts, deafens, blinds, numbs.
A void where?
Empty of what?
I read to fill it. One book after another.

Pell-mell…

Madame Bovary doesn't like her daughter very much…

Is it possible not to like one's children?

Virginia Woolf, who has none,

demands a room of her own

stones in her pockets, she walks into the river.

Penelope carries on with what never ends.

Must one continue?

Books pose too many questions.

I stop reading.

The sun shines, I'm in the dark.

I walk, empty.

I think, empty.

Emptiness surrounds me

weighs on me despite the sun, despite the children, despite
the books.

I must, I tell myself, rid myself of what I am, part with it.

No longer to be?

I cook, I pick at my food, grow thin, pity myself,

a bit like Emma.

I go to see the doctor.

He sounds me, probes my belly, my breasts, talks of lumps,
cancer, removals.

"Oh!" exclaims my Corsican mother-in-law.

"That's too bad," says her son.

A knife in my flesh? That's too bad?

I write to my mother.

"Ah no," she replies, "it's not possible, there's no question,
come to Berlin, we'll see what the specialists say."

The horizon comes back into view.

The egotist mother decides to take care of her body.

"The children will stay here," declares their father. "Who knows what you might come up with so as not to return?"

THE DEPARTURE

We're at the El Aouina airport…
I love that name full of vowels. I love that melodic, lyrical
language, soft to the ear. I love this land, its architecture, its
palm trees, its bougainvilleas with so many shades of pink,
its people.
It's the beginning of summer, the weather is mild, people
are smiling, multi-colored dresses waft in the breeze on the
tarmac.
My sons have taken off their sandals, dip their feet in the
cooling pool of a large fountain with its many jets of water.
They laugh.
Here is the plane I'm going to take.
The two boys, five and seven, look at it
look at me
look at the mother who's leaving
I hold them by their hands, put my arms round them,
kiss them, kiss them again
they smell good
I love their fresh, slim bodies
their brilliant eyes

their voices.
I love them
with all my heart.
Afraid for my body, I board the plane alone
without them
coward that I am
afraid for myself
afraid quite simply of the knife in my flesh.
Could I not have seen another doctor in Tunis?
Would a good mother have left her children? Would she
have entrusted them to that father?
The eldest looks at me.
Silent.
Does he know I won't be coming back?

THE LEAP OF NO RETURN

I didn't know myself. I was going to Berlin to consult an
oncologist, nothing more.

"You're young," he tells me, "there's nothing to worry about.
Like many women your age, you have fibroadenomas
in your breasts, well-defined growths about two or three
centimeters in diameter. They're round, move easily under
the skin, and are firm to the touch. Look, touch yourself
there."

"I…"

He smiles.

"You're self-conscious…"

"Fib…"

"Fibroadenomas… That's all. No danger.

I laugh.

I walk out of his office with a light tread, smiling, happy. I
go home to my parents. We drink tea on the terrace behind
the house, the grass is green, the cherry tree proudly displays
its fruit, the dahlias are in their prime. It's a lovely day. I bask
in my well-being.

Would not a good mother immediately return to her
children?
Me, that night, I sleep in my childhood bedroom
the birch tree branches in front of my window stir, and
caress me
the street lamp, as in the past, casts over me its soft light.
In the morning I go downstairs, I hold tight to the banister
with my right hand, jump the last four steps with my feet
together, as before the war, before being wed, before having
children.
That's when I decide on the divorce.
The children?
My sons loom up before my eyes, I see again the look on
Martin's face at the airport.
It does not occur to me that I could be cut off from my
children.

THE LAW

Theo advises me to see a lawyer.
"It'll take a few months," the man tells me, "but you'll get
custody of your children. Don't worry, be patient. The
divorce will take place here, in Berlin."
He's mistaken.
That same year, 1954, France and Germany sign an
agreement stipulating that a divorce between a Frenchman
and his German wife will take place where the children
reside.
In Tunis, then.
A ceaseless exchange of letters and documents.
Endless discussions.
Weeks pass, then months.
I think of them without being able to improve their lives.
I write to my children — does he give them my letters? — I
send them little gifts, photos, but I have trouble maintaining
regular daily or even weekly contact with two children
too young to carry on alone, without any help, a regular
correspondence.

I don't talk to them. There's no telephone at 43, rue de
Bretagne, where they now live.
I don't know their friends, their teachers, I don't know what
they're learning.
Michel, the little one, has he begun to read?
Are they happy or sad? I know nothing.
Ah! If there were e-mail at the time! Skype!
In 1954, I resign myself to my situation
as a mother far from her children
as a mother having abandoned her children without
knowing
when she would see them again.
"Patience," says the lawyer.
Patience is a gray envelope in which I keep the few photos of
them that I possess.
We don't see each other, we don't hear each other, we don't
touch each other. We are not together.
I am the amputated mother.
How to prevent the good in one's existence from being
snuffed out by the contrary winds of the day-to-day?
I fill my days with study and work.
I flirt.
A man cheers me up.
I reproach myself for it.

*How is it that this man, who has recently suffered the loss of
his only son, and who, beset by trials and quarrels, and this
morning so troubled, thinks no more of it now? Do not be*

astonished: he is entirely preoccupied with noting where that boar will pass, which his dogs have been chasing for the last six hours. It takes no more than this. Man, however afflicted with sadness he may be, if we may entice him into one distraction or another, will show himself to be happy for that length of time; and man, however happy he may be, if he is not diverted by some passion or amusement that prevents boredom from having its way, will soon be ill-humored and unhappy. Without entertainment, there is no joy; with entertainment, there is no sadness.

PASCAL

THREATS

Later I am told that the Corsican grandmother held Martin, the eldest — whom she loved so dearly — by his two hands over the railing of her apartment's little balcony on the third floor of 43, rue de Bretagne, threatening to let him drop if he didn't calm down. Is it true? Recently — he's now sixty-one years old — I asked him the question. He replied that he had no memory of that. Smiling. Happy to have submerged the details of an unhappy childhood.

I am told that he had become a difficult child, tending to wildness, that it was all because of me, his vagabond mother who'd abandoned him, that he stole money from his grandmother's wallet, ate hidden chocolates, put cockroaches in the beds and the pantry, didn't wash his ears, and bit the fingers of the "dirty old" grandmother if she insisted he do so. I can imagine my son defending himself, with his mother absent. I hear him crying:

"No, you won't cut my nails, neither on my hands or my feet, I'll never wear the sweater you're knitting for me, I don't want you to touch me, I hate you, you're ugly, unfair... Wait until my mother comes back..."

"She's not coming back!"

"Liar, dirty liar!"

The child throws a tantrum, the difficult child becomes even more difficult, he's beaten, he's deprived of fruit, he who loves it so much, they again threaten to throw him from the balcony, to call the police, to put him in prison, they say his mother doesn't love him any more, that she'll never return, that he has no more mother.

He hears the threats, the ominous intimations.

There's no one to console him.

There's nowhere for him to hide.

He can't run away.

He doesn't know where his mother is.

He keeps silent.

The other

the younger one

the one who's not difficult

listens

learning over and over again

the he must

keep silent

to survive.

SOMETIMES, PERHAPS, AT NIGHT, THEY TALK

"Martin, are you asleep?"

"No."

"Do you believe what they say?"

"No."

"Do you think she'll come back?"

"I don't know."

"So you believe them?"

"No."

"She was nice."

"Yes."

"She laughed."

"All the time."

"Not all the time."

"Most of the time."

"Tomorrow, maybe?"

"What?"

"She'll come back?"

"I don't know."

"Are you mad at her?"

"No. You?"

"No. Do you think she's mad at us?"

"She would have said so."

"That's true."

1955

It's summer
happy, three times happy!
The mother returns to live with her children
three weeks of happiness in Tunis
in the house a woman offers me
a chance friend
who takes a photo of the two boys and me
three times the same smile on the wide avenue
where they sell the flowers
I once wanted and no longer need.
Finally my sons see their mother
happy and relaxed
in the sun
on the beaches
so white
in the welcoming water of the Mediterranean Sea
that she'll have to re-cross all the same.
"You're going away again, mama?"
"I'll be back at Christmas," she says.

In December, 1955, Tunisia's independence is close at hand. *Bourguiba-Bourguiba* they sing on the beautiful avenue that will bear his name.

The enthusiasm is huge.

The children laugh at me and my suitcase, to which I've tied a Christmas tree.

Michel inspects our room:

"Where are we going to put it?" he asks.

"In front of the wardrobe mirror," replies Martin, "that way we'll see it twice!"

And here we are celebrating Christmas in a hotel room with egg and parsley briks, merguez sausages, German Christmas fruits and biscuits. She is good, this mother who sings

Stille Nicht! Heilige Nacht!
Alled schläft, einsam wacht
Nur das traute hochheilige Paar
Holder Knabe im lockigen Haar

She invents games, takes her sons laughing to the medina, loses herself there with them, runs into the street late at night to find a doughnut seller who's still open.

Bourguiba, Bourguiba. The chant grows louder.

"Take them," says the father, unsettled by his own forced uprooting — a French civil servant, he'll be repatriated to France — "take them to Berlin."

I don't thank him.

I don't ask myself any questions.

I don't think about laws and contracts,

in short I don't worry about anything.
I cart them off, my sons
I cart them off with joy
certain that I'll make my way.

MAKING MY WAY

That means making the impossible possible
supporting the children
while studying
earning enough to live
to give them shelter
to feed them
to laugh with them
sometimes to cry
to clothe them
to take them
to school
to the doctor
to the dentist
later
elsewhere
to pay for their education
in whole
in part
to attend to their needs
since

their father desists
Oh!
sometimes the mother
is tired
exhausted
in debt
but she finds a way
each day
because she must.

BERLIN

In Berlin, my children unlearn their fear. There are no more cries, blows, threats, or punishment. The grandparents are patient. As am I. Oh, the grandfather grumbles when the little Frenchmen, for whom he has bought French bread, don't finish the crusts they've torn off to wipe their plates. But it's not serious. We explain, and then we laugh. It's not much fun either when his grandsons, rather than contenting themselves with the sweetest of fruit from the large plum tree, pluck from the lattice unripe pears he's been cultivating with great care. But in the end, the old man always has a bit of chocolate for them in one of his desk drawers. And they're allowed to interrupt him when they have a question. They just have to knock at the door, and wait for his
Ja?
and the typewriter goes silent.
A curious business, this writing about which he says nothing, but that makes a strong impression on them.
A question, an answer, a piece of chocolate.
A kiss?

"You know, mama, the Germans don't kiss all the time," says Michel.

"They shake hands," Martin explains.

They're adapting, my two Pieds-Noirs.

I enroll them in the French school.

At the ages of eight and ten, they travel alone, on the subway, every day.

Am I asking too much of them?

I imagine them strong and joyful, laughing at all the serious commuters who are telling them to keep quiet.

Ah, the French, it's obvious, they don't know discipline.

I pursue my studies, work as an interpreter, translator, teacher.

Martha, my good mother, is there for the children when I am not.

At school, Michel is well behaved, *as good as gold*, they say.

Martin, writes the headmaster in March, *plays the fool*.

A meeting between the principal — a nervous fellow who can't stop chewing his fingernails — the grandfather, and the mother, while the child waits alone in the corridor for his fate to be determined.

"A restless child," says the principal.

"An intelligent child," says the former professor.

"A difficult child," admits the mother.

"I won't be stupid any more," he promises.

Three months, twelve weeks…

Finally, I'm authorized to enroll my two sons for the following year.

But what will they do during the long summer vacation?

Four weeks in a summer camp recommended by the French consulate will pass quickly.

Shortly after the two children have returned, a young man rings the doorbell.

"It's Stéphane, the counsellor," cries Martin as he lets him in. Why does Michel look so uneasy?

The young man has arrived with an accusation.

"Your sons damaged their tent," he says, "we ended up throwing it away."

"How…"

"Well," says Michel, "it was raining hard, and we just wanted to see what would happen if we made a little hole in the canvas where the rain water was gathering, with our beautiful Swiss knives. You should have seen!"

"We couldn't have known it would flood like that, the sleeping bags all got soaked," adds Martin.

I slip the intruder a few bills. My parents won't know anything about it.

I'm getting a bit tired of my sons' antics. I send them to their room under the roof. Would not a good mother have punished them?

I go up a few minutes later to tell them that in fact that was quite amusing, my two little North Africans under Normandy's summer rain… When I arrive, I see only my older son's hands hanging onto the windowsill:

Martin is suspended over the stone terrace!

Silent, Michel looks at me, as if to say: Do something, mama.

I run down to Theo, explain what's going on, quickly drink the cognac he's holding out to me, go back up with him. Martin obeys the order, firmly delivered by the grandfather, to come back in.

I'm exhausted.

My parents could use less drama in their lives.

ALONE WITH THEM

I rent an apartment in town.
I go on with my studies.
I teach French, part time, in three schools.
I love teaching, even if sometimes, leaving in the morning, I
don't know which direction to take.
We're surviving, I say to myself.
Michel, the wise child, is always serenely happy. He reads.
He writes. He makes up stories.
Martin reads, too. When he runs out of books, he steals
them from a French-German used bookstore near his school.
A child thief?
Should I punish him?
"André Gide did the same thing," Theo tells me.
I love my father, who knows so many things.
I laugh. I love my son who steals books.
My difficult son.
A good mother would have made her son apologize to
the merchant, would have believed that the humiliation
would constitute a lesson for this young person who thinks
anything is permitted him...

But had not Gide, the famous Gide, said that *humiliation, on the contrary, makes one all the more arrogant?*

A bad mother, I place my confidence in the young reader's development.

I visit the shopkeeper, I reimburse him. The man laughs with me:

"Let's hope he'll keep on reading!"

I teach constantly, I lack money, I give private lessons.

Always good, my mother pays for a cleaning lady.

Sunday morning, we cross the Grunewald, spend the day with my parents, return to the apartment, our bellies full, backpacks stuffed with supplies for the days to come, and laundry washed in the maternal washing machine.

Once a week, the difficult child sees a psychoanalyst.

"He doesn't talk much, but he's extremely polite," the doctor tells me.

Because sometimes I go too.

After all, perhaps I'm the difficult one.

ANOTHER EMIGRATION?

1956

Having passed the *Staatsexamen,*[4] I thought of beginning
to teach full time in a Berlin lycée, becoming a bureaucrat
like the others, with a permanent job, a proper salary, paid
insurance and vacations, a pension, security for life. Forget
the little contracts, three hours here and three hours there,
in private schools! An end to the fear of not having enough
money to buy a pair of shoes, a blouse,
perhaps a skirt…

Damn! They tell me that in becoming naturalized as French
so as to be able to teach in Tunisia, I lost my German
nationality, and in order to teach in a German public school,
I'd have to reacquire it:

"Live here five years, and you'll have it!"

Five years?

I've never been patient.

I'm furious.

Divorced at last, but without the question of custody being
resolved, with no maintenance allowance for the children, I

---

[4] An examination that is the equivalent of a Master's.

don't know what to do. I need work, full-time work!

A Canadian friend talks to me about beautiful francophone Quebec, its cities, its lakes, its forests, the two oceans and their coasts...

Eve sends me an ad from the Protestant School Board of Montreal, which is looking for French teachers...[5] She tells me that with my British passport I'd be welcome in Montreal...

Idiot that I am, I advise the father of these possibilities, invite him to come and say good-bye to the children.

The reply?

"Send them to me for a few weeks."

A bad mother, I ask for nothing better, tell myself that I will be free, with fewer meals to prepare, less cleaning to do... That I could go and spend the night with my lover or invite him to sleep in my bed... The idea of some short-term freedom charms me. Four weeks! I'd have the time to prepare our departure for Canada.

"Bon voyage," I say to them, hanging around their necks tickets, passports, etc. "I've talked to the conductor, he'll take care of you. You have sandwiches, apples, chocolate, lemonade. Don't eat everything right away, it's a long trip. And enjoy yourselves..."

It doesn't occur to me that I might be separated from my children.

---

[5] In 1958, the Protestant School Board of Montreal did not have the right to hire Catholic teachers. As there were not many Protestant (or Jewish) teachers who could teach the French language, they went looking for them outside the country.

"I'm keeping them," their father writes me once they've arrived. "They'll never go back to Germany."

Tears.

Despair.

Anger.

How could I have been so naïve?

Theo and I leave for Arras to negotiate my sons' return to Berlin. The analyst's certificate affirms that Martin, a troubled child, must not be separated from his mother.

Two days of negotiation, then:

"Very well," concedes Jean, who seems to have no desire to deal with his difficult child, "take him, but the other one stays here. He adores the bicycle I've just bought him…"

"Who cares about bicycles," says Martin, suddenly eloquent, "if the little twerp wants to stay here for a bicycle, let him, he'll regret it, that's for sure, you'll see."

Michel smiles. A bit embarrassed, perhaps.

At his age, what wouldn't one do to have a shiny new bicycle?[6]

My sons' father is still a member of the French police. I dare not pursue the fight without consulting the lawyer in Berlin. "Patience," he'll tell me.

Alas

for the moment

a long moment

my easy child

who is not rebellious

---

[6] Michel never stopped being a cyclist. After retiring, he crossed Canada by bicycle.

whose residence is now in Arras
in France
remains lost to me.

CANADA WILL WAIT

There will be no ocean voyage this year.
I have to try to keep Martin happy.
For the first time, he's without his brother, who admired
him, followed him, was his close companion.
Here he is alone
with me
nervous
exhausted
constantly in a rush
busy
teaching
studying
earning money
reorganizing our lives
always in a new way.
I find it hard to see him continuing on at the French school,
where the teachers loved Michel and were afraid of his
brother, the clown.
I must have him near me. I'm afraid he'll be taken from me.
I teach French in a Waldorf school whose pedagogy is based

on love, confidence, and enthusiasm, all of which I want to give to my son.

I enroll Martin.

He'll speak German.

The classes for children his age, ten, finish at about one o'clock, and he'll go to have lunch with my parents, who live very near. He'll stay with them until I come to pick him up. We're safe and sound.

UNDER THE EYE OF THE SON

Sitting at the back of the class, Martin's uneasy, he stares at me, sends me messages without saying a word:
Mama! You remember? You asked us to read six pages and to pay attention to the vocabulary! You said there'd be a test, Mama!
I smile at him discreetly.
He defies me.
And here are your pupils reading out loud! Mama! Always changing your plans!
I smile at him, certain he'll understand my answer:
I have whims too
that I need
my son
so forget the test no one wants anyway.

Wednesday evening, we end up in our analyst's waiting room.

MY LITTLE HABITS

Sometimes I allow myself to be lazy.
It's not something I plan.
People fall ill
fall in love
become pregnant
sometimes I lapse into laziness
it's when I no longer want to do what I've planned
when Martin is busy
happy
secure
asleep
work is all done
or almost
I take a book, a novel, maybe some knitting
I need a soft chair
the pink armchair near the window
ergonomic, comfortable
"Dare to be lazy," counsels Barthes.
When I work, read, inform myself
when I write

I pay no attention to my body's comfort.
Sitting in the armchair
yoked to my desk
and later at my computer
I lose track of my body.
A bad habit? So be it.
I love to work,
at my ease or not.
But laziness means comfort, at least for me.

SLEEP

When really
I can do no more
when it's late
and my words, sentences
legs and arms
become heavy
when my eyes close
there's only one solution:
I go to bed.
The bad mother
disconnects
goes to sleep like a baby
sleeps like a dormouse
or rather like a marmot
the sleep of the just.

SEXUALITY

It's not because I live
single
a single mother
that sex doesn't exist for me.
Without sexuality, there's no history, says Kierkegaard.
And no life, I tell myself, the philosopher providing me with
a good excuse.
My only concern is not to trouble my son.
Love
desire
of the moment
or for a time
love and what goes with it
its preambles
its postscripts
occurs when Martin is at school and I am not.
It's simple.
There's the man of the theater for whom the hour is ideal
the man of law whose time is his own
the student who is always free

the analyst who often is not
the Canadian friend
married and father of six...
Except for the student, they're all married
one like another
these men I frequent.
There's never a question of marriage
the very idea terrifies me.
Once I find myself pregnant, and I abort
while Martin's at school.
Bad mother...
Enough, let's say no more about that.

CATASTROPHE

Whose idea was this puppy called Érémentia?
Where did we find that little animal with its long thin legs?
I've totally forgotten, and I don't want to ask Martin, who
might, even today at his advanced age, vent all his anger on
me. His despair.
Ah no, I wasn't in the midst of making love when the
veterinarian euthanized the sick dog, when my father threw
his terrible tantrum on learning that the dog had been
buried in the garden; I was somewhere in a school.
The accident happened at night. We'd had Érémentia for a
week. Martin was holding her in his arms when she broke
free and jumped to the ground.
A fractured foreleg. An improvised dressing with wrappings
and spatulas. The next day, fever, diarrhea, vomiting.
I take Martin and his dog in a taxi to my mother, who'll find
a veterinarian, then I'm off to my mandatory job.
"It's two stops away," she tells Martin, "you get off — you
have to carry her — you leave the station…"
"You're not coming?"

"I can't, dear. I'm not feeling well this morning, my right leg, you know… And I have to make jam, I repeat, you go out of the station, you turn right, you'll see the clinic. I've phoned, they'll see Érémentia right away…they'll probably keep her for the day. Tonight, we'll go and get her. With your mother."

Martin looks at the veterinarian, who explains that the animal, not yet vaccinated, is suffering from a serious illness, a parvovirus. She'll have to be put to sleep. There. Now.

"When will she wake up?"

Damn, the veterinarian must have thought, why did this family send me a young boy all by himself with his dog that's about to croak? Idiots? Delinquents?

"She's not going to wake up. She's going to die from that sickness. This needle I'm going to give her will help her…"

"To die?"

"Yes. My assistant will give you a blanket to wrap her in, you can take her home, it will be like she's asleep."

I imagine Martin in the subway, the motionless dog under the blanket, my son's face.

"We'll bury her in the garden," says my mother, "over there, at the back, then you'll make her a pretty grave, with flowers, pansies perhaps…"

After the ceremony, they have lunch on the terrace. Grandfather arrives.

"Is Martin sick?" he asks, "or is he playing hooky? Where is his little friend with the funny name, though it's pretty?"

Martin bursts into tears, he wants to show Theo the grave, but he, like a true patriarch, becomes unimaginably angry:

"In my garden? Under the plum tree? To feed the plums? So we can eat them afterwards? But damn it all, you're completely crazy! It's out of the question! You hear me? It's forbidden to bury animals in gardens, didn't you know that? It's illegal. *Verboten!* And if one of the neighbors had seen?" Martha tries to calm him. Martin cries.

"And you're crying? You'll have to start over! Right now. You'll dig up your Érémentia, you'll bury her somewhere else, and you'll stop blubbering, that doesn't do anyone any good, your mother never should have bought you that dog, she lays everything on our doorstep when things go wrong… *Verdammt noch mal!* That's all I need, the police in my garden…"

The dog exhumed, there is Martha, a shovel under her arm, Martin with Érémentia in a basket, en route for Grunewald, in search of a spot with lots of moss where they'll make a soft bed for the poor creature.

Oh! How furious I was with my father!

CANADA?

Martha encourages me to go:
"I'll come to see you both, Eve, you, your sons..."
Really? She' suffering from an illness that's slowly paralyzing
her... I shouldn't leave her, I know.
But I'm tempted.
Ghana, Estonia, Japan, Italy, England, Germany, Austria,
Australia, Tunisia, the United States, Canada... My family's
made up of people who've lived all over, travelers unfazed by
foreign parts...
Canada...
The friend tells me about his cottage on the shore of a big
lake
and fires around which people talk, at night...
The school board offers me a contract...
But to leave the continent where Michel is living?
To write him from Berlin, to write him from Montreal,
what's the difference...
I mull things over.
It's not a question of letter writing.
It's a question of distance.

Of immediate help, if necessary.
Of my child's well-being.
We haven't seen each other for over a year
his father has no telephone.
When I ask my lawyer where we stand, he counsels patience.
I ought to take the train
go and see if everything's all right.
I have no money.
It's an excuse that doesn't hold water.
If I asked them, my parents would give it to me, the damned money.
A bad mother, I didn't go to see my son Michel. I continued to argue with myself, and then I left.

GANDER, MAY 1958

I no longer remember why our plane made a stop at Gander. What I do remember is that Martin made the rounds of the waiting room, inspecting the bottles of Coca Cola that people had left half-empty on the tables, and finished them off with pleasure. I smiled as I watched my son relishing a drink I didn't usually buy him. And apparently I had no fear of germs.

"This must be a rich country, Canada," he said.

Rich because people didn't finish the drinks they bought? With me, you always finished what was on your plate or in your glass.

A rich country, with an abundance of Coca Cola?

A happy arrival, in any case, a favorable first impression.

MONTREAL

As for me, things, as they say, could have been worse. The Canadian lover picked me up at Eve's the evening we arrived in Montreal, and took me up on the mountain to where there's a magnificent panoramic view of the city. We walked off a few meters, and behind a bush of some sort, made passionate love.
I asked nothing
he promised nothing
but through the evening, under a starry sky, just like that, surrounded by nature, above the city lit by millions of lighted windows, we shared some magic moments that I, in any case, have never forgotten.

PENNILESS IMMIGRANTS

We arrived in the month of May.

Our trip was paid for by the Protestant School Board of Montreal, and in addition, by my father, who didn't know we were getting a free ride.

And so thanks to him, and without his knowing it, I had a few hundred dollars, enough to pay for one or two months of rent, two beds, two pillows, sheets, a sofa, a table, a few chairs, some dishes, some pots and pans, and some modest provisions, while waiting for the month of September and my first regular cheque.[7]

Oh! How I hate talking about money.

All my life

or almost

I was chasing after the sums I needed to support my children, without receiving any alimony from anyone, chasing after degrees that held out some promise of a decent income.

---

[7] A salary of $4,800 dollars per year, $400 per month, with the usual deductions.

In June 1958, in Montreal, I became a saleswoman in a record store on Sherbrooke Street:

"You're of German origin, Madame? So you know classical music."

As in the Tunisian high school!

"That will be $35 a week."

August: housed and fed, a counsellor for a theater program in a camp for young girls.

I like sleeping in a tent, I like being outside.

I breathe easy.

On the other hand, Martin, sent off during this time to a Red Feather camp, has an unpleasant time of it.

So as not to worry me, he says nothing, explains nothing.

A PACT

As far as I know
there was no pact
but perhaps an understanding
between my two sons
and later my daughter:
Silence,
we have to protect mama.
Thus
my three musketeers
for whom, in a way, I'm writing these books
have
from the beginning
and up to the present day
without telling me
— I don't know why —
taken me for a weakling who needs protection
from any misfortune
any reverse
and any affront
while I considered myself

responsible for their well-being.
It's very nice to know yourself loved.

CUSTOMS AND SURPRISING LAWS

Martin had attended lay French schools, public and therefore free. First in Tunisia, then in Berlin. After his return from Arras, I'd enrolled him in Berlin's Waldorf School, a private lay school where as a teacher I didn't have to pay his tuition. In Canada, I discover that religion, education and language are inseparable...
In Montreal, beautiful and modern, there is no lay public school, neither in French nor in English.
An atheist like my parents, am I going to put my francophone child into a Catholic school?
The idea seems absurd to me.
Or in an anglophone Protestant school?
I teach there, I enroll him there, in the end that's what's simplest.
In any case, I don't have the money to send him to a private school, and besides, my grandparents were Protestants.

In September, I enroll in the University of Montreal to prepare a doctorate in French literature. I find myself in a sea

of soutanes, white veils, and black habits worn by the other
students, of which few are women.

The first course is given by Brother M., who begins by going
on his knees before us, then reciting a long prayer.

And what to make of this unforgettable literature professor,
a gentleman of unmistakeably French origin, who, before
delivering his Saturday morning lecture, recites the Lord's
Prayer at a surprising, and joyously dazzling speed?

In the library, the books on the Index are marked with a
little red star.

Curious phenomena
that will do me no harm.

THREE LITTLE TRICKS

He had plenty of them up his sleeve, did Martin.

I only remember three.

One Friday morning I'm not at school, I have a cold, I'm half asleep, the telephone rings.

"Madame, do you have a twelve-year-old son, Martin?"

"Yes sir. What…"

"It's the police station. Your son…"

"He's hurt? He…"

"He's been taking the money that housewives leave in bottles on their doorsteps for the milkman… We've brought him to the station, Madame."

They give me the address, I throw on my clothes, I hurry over.

Martin is sitting in the main office. A bit pale. Happy to see me.

"I didn't know the money was to buy milk…"

It ended there. There were no consequences. I explained to him that there was a sort of contract between the milkman and the housewives, that he, Martin, was wrong to think that that was money nobody wanted…

I could have punished him, read him paragraphs from the penal code, recited the Ten Commandments.
I did nothing of the sort, I told him it was very disagreeable to be wakened by the police.

A little later, there was the fire.
It was summer, the vacation is long. Martin and Johnny, Eve's son, are bored. One afternoon, they decide to make a picnic in a vacant lot, a real Canadian picnic, with hot-dogs and marshmallows to grill, things easy to find in Eve's kitchen. They need something to make a fire: matches also from the kitchen, then, picked up on the way, bits of paper, twigs, little pieces of dry wood, a few larger pieces of wood. The fire takes, and they grill the hot-dogs, swallow them almost unchewed, stick the marshmallows onto long branches, oh, they're going to be good! But the police are already there to teach them a lesson: no, even in Canada, you can't light a fire just anywhere, get into the car, you're lucky we're not putting you in handcuffs, we're taking you back to your parents.

A year later, the police bring him back from Mount Royal — we're now living in the city — where he went to chase squirrels with his Daisy Red Ryder BB-gun, bought from a friend. Without telling me, of course. Who would have let his mother in on such a thing, when many mothers are speaking out against such purchases?[8]

This image: me, thanks to the Nazis, wary of any man in a uniform, mother of a child who'd never possessed a toy bearing any likeness to a weapon, begging the police officers not to charge my son, but rather to get rid of the Daisy Red Ryder, of whose potential he's completely ignorant:

"I thought it was just a toy!"

I always believed in his innocence.

---

[8] Between 1950 and 2013, more than 10 million of these weapons for young people were sold. Today, Canadian Tire sells them for $64.99 each.

ABANDONED

I spend forty hours a week at school teaching French to
anglophones who for the most part have no interest in
learning it. The textbook used by the Protestant School
Board is inspiring for no one.
At university, I take courses much like those I've already
followed in Berlin.
I could have found the time to write to Michel during these
repetitive sessions, but, bad mother, it doesn't even occur to
me.
The young cyclist in Arras
has no news of me most of the time.
Far from him
I am unconcerned about him
assuming foolishly that his father is caring for him
as I care for Martin.
Sometimes I send him a little message
that gets no answer
which seems almost normal to me.
The idea that the father might mistreat this good student
who is so well-behaved, who always does his homework and

keeps his room in order, doesn't even enter my mind.
How stupid could I be!
If only there had been e-mail at the time!
Skype!
If only I'd been a better mother
attuned to the here
and the far away!
But what with the close-to-home, the immediate, the
day-to-day,
the accumulation of my most trivial concerns
I lost track
of my second son.
Today, "I drink the bitter cup of expiation."[9]

---

[9] Balzac.

DISTRACTIONS

The Canadian friend takes me to New York for a weekend,
then to Quebec City, but what are two weekends when the
year contains fifty-two?

I meet a young writer who later will sing the praises of older
women in a book. As if she'd never had an affair, Eve frowns,
but takes care of Martin during my escapades.

"Just marry your businessman," she tells me.

I laugh, tell her about his six children, their mother:
"You understand?"

Should I set off in search of another man, different,
marriageable?

Towards the end of the school year, I meet Amadeus, a
Dane, a French teacher, also an immigrant.

He's good-looking, he pleases me, he resembles Steve
McQueen, Michelangelo's *David*.

Amadeus? Loved by God?

Why should I not love him?

Two weeks of seeing each other, and he moves in with me.

Martin's not surprised.

Is he happy with this male presence?

Happy for me, perhaps?
In any case, something new comes into our lives.
Camping.
Fishing.
One lovely summer morning, somewhere in the Laurentians,
Martin, laughing, brings me his first trout. Today, still, he
enjoys his rod and reel.

Yet he doesn't laugh when he has to wait in the car while
his mother's boyfriend makes himself presentable in a gas
station toilet, when this man who's moved in with us comes
to occupy more and more space.
Bad mother, I'm oblivious.

GREAT IS MY DEVOTION

Amadeus dreams:

"I'd like to enroll in university, do a Master's…earn more…"

"I'll help you…"

"You'll have to teach me how to write a thesis…"

"I'll write it for you."

In short, Amadeus absorbs me.

"An apartment nearer to the university would be practical," he says, not for a moment considering that that would distance Martin from his cousin and his Aunt Eve, whom he loves, that he would then be terribly alone. And I, bad mother, don't think about it either:

"Let's do it," I say, submissive as I have never been.

Once the lease is signed, I come back to earth: the apartment has only one bedroom… How did I not see that Martin wouldn't have his own room? It's true that I've just enrolled him as a boarder in a lycée at the other end of the island, but to deprive him of a family home?

I must have been mad.

In love to the point of forgetting Martin as I forgot Michel.

121

❀

Usually my memory is good, but today, July 4, 2013, in my
little office in Toronto, I can't remember the name of the
Montreal boarding school where I placed Martin during
the week, because I was tired of him, and smitten with my
Danish lover.

I don't remember the institution's name, but I remember the
Sunday nights: Amadeus, my son and I, in the car, en route
for East Montreal and its huge oil refineries, the largest in
Canada, where the air quality is the worst on all the island
of Montreal and in Quebec, where the sky is a Dantesque,
infernal red.

That's where I took my child, the poorly loved.

And so today
I sought the institution's name
on line
for hours
and details on what his life must have been
just five days a week
but that in no way changes
nor in any sense diminishes my guilt.
It's somewhere
in Pointe-aux-Trembles
that I had my son live
five days a week
so I could live without him.
I remember another Sunday night
— already the tears come to my eyes —
which will not lessen my shame

crying makes no difference
the facts are the facts
and add up to
the bad mother I was.
For some reason, we couldn't return him to Pointe-aux-
Trembles that night.
I went down with him to the bus stop, I kissed him, then
went back up to the apartment.
Someone was crying down below, on Boulevard de
Maisonneuve
I knew it was Martin
howling out
all his rage
all his unhappiness
all his solitude.
I didn't go back down.
And he didn't come up
he returned to the school to which I'd condemned him.

The institution discovers that Martin has written to an
American criminal, condemned to death, to tell him how
much he admires him; the principal phones me, threatens
to expel him. Breathlessly, I tell the man how hard I work,
am able to persuade him to keep my son until the end of the
school year.
Martin thinks he has a right to his opinions
tells me so
and I don't contradict him.

I write to Theo who replies that the young man
is a romantic like so many others.
I no longer believe in his solace.
I'd like to cover myself with ashes.

THE ADVENTURERS

We are offered two positions at the University of Addis Ababa.

The adventure suits us.

Requirements: a marriage, and a finished thesis.

An impassioned lover, I write my lover's Master's thesis.

I'm in no rush for my doctorate, I'll work things out, I'm used to that.

Martin seems happy for me and for himself.

In August, we'll take the plane for Addis Ababa.

Now Martin refuses to go along with the adventure.

Can we take him by force to Africa, a fourteen-year-old boy who's fed up with the perturbations his mother has forced on him?

Eve promises to take care of Martin. He himself remembers a farm in the Eastern Townships where he spent a weekend with his cousin: the Eastern Townships are lovely and peaceful, the farmwife gentle, the husband also.

"That's where I want to stay, finish high school, live in peace."
Is that perhaps convenient for me as well?

A SLAP

"Martin needs a winter coat," Eve decides, "take him to Ogilvy's."
I'm not enthusiastic about spending the money, Martin doesn't want a coat.
"None of my friends has one, it's a European thing."
We go anyway to the favorite store for anglophone shoppers, with elevator ladies in white gloves.
My son isn't happy there.
I buy him an expensive green and brown Scottish woollen overcoat, knowing he'll never wear it.
We quarrel on the way down the great marble staircase, the sulking son and the exasperated mother who gives him a slap.
It's the first time I've lost control that way.
Buying a coat will not excuse my lack of sensitivity towards my son. I should have known that he didn't want that cursed coat, that he wanted despite everything to go away with me, just like his brother in Arras...

I ought to have posed the question instead of hitting him. For a long time the garment lay around the basements of the houses in which we lived here and elsewhere, reminding me of the slap delivered on Ogilvy's staircase.

MY MOTHER DIES

Increasingly paralyzed, Martha dies in Berlin. I ought to go, right away, but I don't know how to fit this obligation, no, this necessity, this desire, into the long list of my obligations: teaching, end-of-year exams to prepare and correct, report cards to write, Martin's move to organize, our departure for Africa... A pragmatic egoist, I do not rush to my mother's side, I do not enter her hospital room, I do not hold her hand, I am not there for the death of the one who was always there for me.

Martha is dead.

I weep.

Amadeus, who cannot bear my tears, takes me to the movies. I don't know what film we saw, I wept from beginning to end.

I take no leave, I board no plane...

Besides, where to find the money to pay for the return flight?

Always the same excuse...

I ask Christa to delay the burial of the ashes until I can be
there, in August, for a stopover during the flight paid for by
Haile Selassie University.
Pathetic creature.
I've lost my mother,
one son in France
another in Canada
myself adrift
chasing after adventure…

I didn't yet know that the dead, those we've truly loved, stay
with us forever.

EN ROUTE

Amadeus goes to see his parents in Denmark, I travel to
Arras.
Here is my son:
Happy to see me?
Bad mother, I suspect nothing
insensitive mother
I don't divine the secret
the guilt
this child's fear
the unhappiness with which my son is grappling
whether to betray the father
and his morbid fury
whether to remain loyal
or to lay himself bare
and ask for help.
Fear of rejection?
Fear of consequences?
Until he whispers:
"Papa beats me."
I take him in my arms, useless for so long.

"At night, I have to go up to my room, get undressed, lie down on my stomach."

The innocent child is ashamed.

"I have to wait for him."

I relive his fear.

"Then, the belt…"

The tears flow.

How could I not know?

"Take me with you, mama!"

I run, I find a lawyer, meet with a children's judge, a lively woman who, laughing, simply advises me to kidnap the twelve-year-old boy.

"Is he still there on your passport? Yes? There's no problem. Take a train, take a plane, rent a car… Leave!"

The escape succeeds. The Ethiopian adventure can begin.

Will I be a good mother at last?

1961, ADDIS ABABA

First the eucalyptus:
In the morning when I wake
the air seems blue
tinged with the foliage of those trees that rise up everywhere
twenty meters high or more.
In the African city's sky
I see their silhouettes with supple, mobile crowns
sway
substance of shadow and light
their ever-present scent reminding me
oh the miracle
of time recaptured and Boukornine
its cyclamens, the Persian incense of Meriem
nature's beauty
a cliché
until you're gripped by it.

A HAPPY LIFE

The younger son regained. A husband. A good salary. A few
hours of teaching each week, a cook, a maid, a gardener who
takes care of hundreds of multi-colored zinnias flowering
in our garden. The huge tortoise that has agreed to share its
space with us, guards it jealously, hisses a warning when we
get too close.
The vultures in the tops of the eucalyptuses, jealous of the
little biscuits we dip in our tea.
Luxury.
Accustomed to earning a pittance here, a pittance there,
I fret no more about making ends meet.
My thesis on the theater of Paul Claudel in Germany doesn't
excite me, but I'm making progress all the same. Theo sends
me references, doesn't allow me to fritter my time away.
Martin?
I know he's safe.
How is it that I don't ask him to join us?
You'd think that one son was enough for me.
We're living the adventure without Martin.

THE AMPUTATED HAND

Every day
in front of our house
where we are protected by a solid barrier, plus a guard and
other employees,
I see women walking with bent backs
carrying heavy faggots, branches and leaves
from the country to the city
firewood for their cooking.
At night, coming home from a movie
I see on my side of the car
red light bulbs
scraps of red rag over doors
an invitation for men to buy themselves a beer
and a woman's body.
Famine and poverty
seen in Ethiopia
where we live comfortably
amazed
at the misery of others
shocked

by the fact that they've cut off the hand of a man
who committed a wretched theft in the vain hope
of amassing some valueless wealth.
We take photos of this and that
buy an object or two
later to be coated in dust.
To what purpose, the adventure?

NIGHT

Sometimes
at night
the roaring of the emperor's lions wakes me
in Addis Ababa
the cries of hyenas in search of carrion
forgotten in a corner of the city
sometimes it's my mistakes that torment me,
pursue me into the darkest corners of dreams
that I'd prefer to be carefree
in short
my conscience makes itself heard.
Martin's absence weighs on me
I don't write him regularly
my son taking refuge
from his mother's follies
in the Eastern Townships of Quebec
far, far
I live without him
as I've lived without his brother.
And suddenly I want to give birth to another child.

Twice pregnant, twice I miscarry.
Addis Ababa is two thousand five hundred meters in altitude
my body lacks oxygen.
I persevere for a whole year
insist that Amadeus seize the opportunity
when according to the thermometer
it's a propitious moment
even if he doesn't want a child.
Blood loss
needles and pills
the premature birth of a daughter
forevermore the focus of my attention.

1963 AGAIN

That year
my father dies
simply
of a brief bronchitis.
He'd aged
I'd seen him
one last time
in Berlin
on my way to Ethiopia
a brief stopover…
Nevermore will I be able to ask him a question,
he who understood me is no longer there.

PRECIOUS SCISSORS

Return to Montreal
via Berlin
another stopover
one night spent
in the old house
a few souvenirs hastily gathered up
the scissors
for example
taken from one of his desk drawers
the one on the left
I remember
where he also kept the stamps
for the letters he wrote me.
He'll write me no more.

ALONE

I am the daughter of no one
alone
even with the children.
Three children, that's not bad.
And even, in time
with spouses and offspring
they'll be seventeen
and more.
But today
February 4, 1963
the day of my father's death
I find myself at the top
of the familial ladder
my breath stopped.
Michel looks at me closely
asks himself
when I too will be gone
as when I left from El Aouina.
The world is precarious.

The wires
sing in the wind.

SUMMER 1963

The man with the beautiful first name is driving the family
Volvo,
I'm sitting beside him, while Marianne, six months, Martin,
seventeen years old, and Michel, fifteen, are in the back.
The road is taking us from Montreal to Grand Forks, North
Dakota, two thousand and eighty-seven kilometers.
No more separation,
my children and I are together.
For good.
Completely.
As if we'd never been separated.
The two brothers have a sister.
Amadeus, is he part of this family?
Seven years younger than me, has he married my past along
with me?
He'll leave us one day.
Once in Grand Forks, each of us will have a role to play:
Amadeus and I will be the breadwinners, Martin and Michel
will go to high school, Marianne will grow.
Life will be happy.

THE END OF THE EVENING

Three hours a day, from nine o'clock to midnight, I work on
my thesis in the tiny office the University of North Dakota
has allotted me in its main library.
To leave this office
alone
so late
the keys between the fingers of my right hand
as I've been taught in the self-defence course
each night I tremble
cross the floor
holding myself erect
as if nothing could happen
yet I'm alert to the killer behind one bookshelf
after another
hear breathing that is not there
one step
and another
I take the elevator
fear the one who will perhaps
get on to join me

no, there's no one
lucky again
I tremble
leave the building
see the invisible rapist in the parking lot
find the car, finally
check the rear seat
what would I do if there were someone there
but there's nobody
I open the door
throw myself onto the seat
head towards our American bungalow.
Breathe.
I see my daughter asleep in her little bed
cover her gently
say goodnight to my sons
have a glass of wine with my handsome husband
in the romantic light of a candle.
Often, we make love.

THE CLOWNS

One freezing afternoon, 30 degrees below, Celsius,
despite the blue sky and the sun
I've just done some errands
I see Michel naked
totally naked
bare-assed
dancing in the snow covering the lawn in the front of the
house
and the other
Martin
threatening him with a knife
not wanting to let him back in the house.
What's going on?
I get out of the car
fast
the second slap of his life
startles Martin
Michel goes into the house
Amadeus is in his darkroom
curious

the little one sits up in her baby chair.
Michel's no longer naked.
The knife is back in the drawer.
And we laugh our heads off.
It was just a joke...

MARTIN'S ADVENTURES

Who told me? Michel?
Would he betray his brother? No.
Amadeus?
His words would have triggered a family drama, with cries
and tears. He preferred to remain silent, to say nothing, to
let things take their course.
A neighbor or someone else?
They don't know me.
The old car parked at the end of the street,
the big brown Chevrolet
so old
so ugly
belongs to Martin.
My son, eighteen years old, owns a car?
That's America, North Dakota.
I should have known
should have remembered that winter day in Montreal
our first winter in that frigid land
when he told me he'd be going to church on Sunday
because that would enable him to play basketball

on Saturday
in the same church's basement.
The church and basketball
that can do no harm, he told me.
I didn't then suspect
how North American customs would take over his life.
In Grand Forks, when my sons started to earn money,
50 cents an hour, clearing and cleaning restaurant tables,
I didn't grasp that this held out a promise
of future wealth.
But didn't he have better things to do at night?
How many weeks did he have to work
to be able to buy the Chevrolet?
Poor Martin
with no driver's license
no insurance
confronting his furious mother
a mother responsible for any potential accident.
Responsible also for the debt incurred at a jeweler's by the
future self-made man
in purchasing an engagement ring
for a sixteen-year-old girl.
A story passed on to me by the young girl's sensible mother
and which was resolved by the two mothers' visit to the
jeweler.
Poor Martin.
Should I have supported him in his desire for independence?
Was I wrong to make clear to him the eventual
consequences?

At the time
I was just
angry.
I didn't understand that a new relationship between mother
and son
was in the works.
A more distant relationship
the son revolting
the mother critical of her son's behavior.
Less laughter
fewer words
the other son in the background of the family portrait
an acute observer
a little girl
exploring her surroundings
the father photographing beauty and ugliness
the mother determined
all the same
to make everyone work together
one for all and all for one.

WHAT A SITUATION!

My father often said:
Mach nichts nur halb,
do nothing by halves…
A family
a thesis
on which I labor
late into the night
the daughter sleeping
the father in his darkroom
me in the library
the sons working at night
in American restaurants
steaks, hot dogs, hamburgers, fries
and Coca Cola…
Dedicated to my children
to the man with whom
at night
I make love
I don't understand that
the eldest needs to escape.

After eighteen years
I, always working
busy with so many things
I should have seen it in his blue eyes
but I was reading
rereading
correcting this damn thesis
on Claudel in Germany
soon to be finished
published
deposited in libraries
in Grand Forks and elsewhere
in Europe
in North America
where young people work at night
in restaurants
to buy a car
a ring
dreams.

THE OBLIVIOUS MOTHER

Tired of everything
of this life of domestic duties, studies and theses
of love and sex
of this Grand Forks
where near the high school
they've set up
recruitment centers
where young boys
turn into soldiers.
I didn't see them, these centers,
me, the oblivious mother.
If only I'd seen them, I'd have been able to talk to him
to talk also to him who was observing his brother
the youth who wanted to sign up
to know danger in the world of men.
I saw nothing.
Just tired
exhausted
persuaded that family life would continue as before
I slept.

But the day he turns eighteen
a Thursday
June 11, 1964
in Grand Forks, North Dakota
Martin enrolls in the American army
raises his right hand
repeats after the sergeant
the words of an oath
that will free him from his mother
and will make him an obedient soldier.

THE SOLDIER'S MOTHER

These centers surrounded the school
on every street corner
no, I hadn't seen them
hadn't understood that they were poised to swallow up
the young man I still thought was my son.
"Let it go," says Amadeus, "he'll learn discipline,"
— as if I'd never taught him anything.
I had no more father to write to
no mother always there to help
to rekindle in my son's eyes
his caring gaze of the avenue Bourguiba.
My son, soldier
sent to Fort Bragg
Fort Hood
and Fort who-knows-what.
Forts filled with young people
preparing for a war on the ground
learning to kill efficiently
acting on orders
as they say.

At the eight-week boot camp
forced marches
the use of arms, of grenades
while bombs are falling on Vietnam
and the infantry is priming for the assault.
There will be a hundred and twenty-five thousand in April
1965
including my son
an apprentice killer.
Did he pass through Fort Poll
known as Tigerland
did he chant
"Kill Kill Kill?"

THE SOLDIER'S DEPARTURE

1965. Back in Montreal.
The soldier's mother demonstrates
the soldier heads for Vietnam.
He'll have two weeks' leave
before his departure
two weeks
is nothing
compared
to eighteen years of his life.
She who defended the infant against bed bugs
goes to the American consulate, asks that they toss the oath
he took
to the winds
his promise to take part in a war that is not his own.
"Why yes, madam," says the consul, "he just has to make a
request…"
"A request is easy to make," I tell my son
who digs in his heels
talks of soldierly honor

of a commitment he's made
refuses.
The day before his departure,
he locks the door of his room
for this last night.
And the mother
the mother who wears buttons proclaiming *Peace*
goes down to the basement
in search of a piece of wood
an iron bar
or a baseball bat
convinced that the only way
to stop her child from going to war
would be to break his leg
crack!
and then
a plaster cast…
She goes back up
the chosen weapon in her hand
realizing at the same time
that she can't hurt her son.
"Amadeus, could you…"
Amadeus says no.
Michel keeps silent.
In the morning
Martin smiles, says he knew it all along,
and goes off to war.
The mother weeps.
She writes to the military authorities, a doctor friend

draws up a certificate saying she's on the verge
of a nervous breakdown, letters pass through the many stages
of bureaucratic transmission, the dossier grows.
One fine morning, in Vietnam, the captain of an infantry regiment opens it,
calls the soldier whose name is Martin, says to him:
"Your mother is worried, she's suffering, she could become ill…"
"My mother is strong, captain," says the soldier, "I know her, there's nothing to these stories of a nervous breakdown."
In short, the soldier refuses to be saved.
He writes many short letters
declaring that everything's going well,
that in fact he's on a beautiful beach
guarding munitions
hands the letters to a friend who works at the military post
for him to send them
to 47, avenue Mariette, in Montreal.
The mother reads them
believes what he says
as she always has
until the day
when she sees that the soldier's brother
receives other letters
mailed from a different address
and realizes
that the munitions on the beach are a lie
invented to pacify her

that her son
is waging war in the Mekong Delta.
For a whole year
day after day
she receives
the lying letters
written out of love and concern.

I SHOULD HAVE…

The night before he left
yes, I should have broken his leg
I should have
nailed boards
over his bedroom window
and across the door as well
I should have assembled the mothers of those
who had done as he did
young Canadians who went off to Vietnam
at the age of eighteen
to embark on
a planned suicide
the mad vision of a heroic death
of decorations and a spectacular career…
I should have tried
to rally these mothers
together we would have stopped them
from making war.
Despairing of my son

I didn't think
of the sons of others
I wept in my own corner
with my weak voice
that I thought had no echo.
We don't know how many Canadians fought in Vietnam
ten thousand, the historians say
thirty thousand, others claim.
Seven vanished
a hundred and three went to their death.
Thirty years later, in 1995, the North Wall,
a commemorative monument dedicated to Canadian
veterans of the Vietnam War, was inaugurated in Windsor,
Ontario.

WARRIOR'S RETURN

My eldest son was lucky.
He returned
as he had left
he wasn't wounded
he completed his studies
he made a career
established a family
raised three girls
who will not go to war.
One day perhaps
we'll talk
of all that
to conclude
as did Pierre Corneille so long ago
in this beautiful line of verse:
And the war ended for lack of combatants.

TIGHT CIRCLE

In Montreal
we live on the top floor of a duplex
near the Loyola campus
where Michel is studying
French literature
where his mother and Amadeus
teach what he's studying.
In the morning
we head out in the same direction.
At night we retrace our steps
almost
together.
We eat
what Betty
Marianne's Austrian minder
has prepared for us.
Her potato salad is excellent,
her Viennese escalope also.
The circle is a bit tight
it's true.

I don't see it.
Martin's kind letters
are not yet lies.
Should I not have remembered that at the age of eighteen
you want to fly the nest?

THE EXCURSION

In the middle of the night, late winter
the telephone rings
I wake
it's the tenant downstairs
my good friend Jackie:
"Marguerite! I don't know what's going on, but I saw a
suitcase tied to some sheets being lowered to the ground
from your floor…"
Quickly
I go down
here in the alley
is my second son, eighteen years old as well, suitcase in hand
on his way to the bus station
to follow in his brother's footsteps.
There are no recruitment centers in Montreal
but I know
and he knows it too
you can find them along the border
between the United States and Canada…
Did he say good-bye?

I don't remember.
I was in a rush to nip in the bud
his dire stratagem.
Poor Michel, it's not funny to be caught
by his mother who
after having gathered up the white sheets
writes on the advice of the American consul
a letter
a copy of which will go to all the recruitment centers
especially the one in Grand Forks, North Dakota
informing them that
if ever
a young Canadian
were to present himself to them
with a letter apparently signed by his mother
authorizing them to enroll him in the American army
this signature would be forged.
Poor Michel
life isn't easy
when you're only eighteen
when you want to go to war
but you're too young
and you need your parents' permission
and you're told
at the Grand Forks recruitment center
that your mother won't allow it.

ZINC IN FLIN FLON

Furious
the young man
hits the road towards Manitoba
hitch hiking
as far as Flin Flon
a name that probably pleased him.
He'll work for Inco Inc.
or another mining company
will muscle up underground
dig up minerals
drink beer
get a tattoo on his left arm
from an inferior artist
a pathetic war emblem
more permanent than the mines
more permanent than
the cannabis plantations
done away with by the government
in Flin Flon

where this medicinal plant grows
between 2002 and 2009.
Strange name
Flin Flon
a place that Michel will leave behind him
after three months.

TRAVELER'S RETURN

Here he is
back in the duplex
in his room at the end of the hall.
Uncommunicative
he sets up a TV
its screen soon swarming with images
and sound effects
gunfire and explosions
designed to conjure the climate of war
bombing
and combat
firearms or knives.
Hideous.
Day and night, war rages at 47 avenue Mariette
noisy
until the day
at last
when the warrior mother
she too

invades this hell
and proclaims in her loudest voice
that this must end
that he turn off the set
that he find a job while waiting to resume his studies
after a year lost
and he does it.
So he's back in the fold, like Nathan Putman's salmon
in *GuruMéditation:*[10] "We think that when the juvenile
salmon leave the river system to enter the ocean, they record
the magnetic field's imprint. It becomes a proxy for the
geographical location when they return as adults."
The imprint of a magnetic field?
Or a Viennese escalope?
A voice, perhaps? A photo? A bed?
I imagine my sons on their road home.
Fortunately, it didn't take them years,
as it does with the salmon, to reach adulthood.

---

[10] http://gurumed.org/2013/02/09

ALL IS WELL

Michel, also, returned safely
completed his studies
made a career
founded a family
raised three girls
and a boy
who
to date
just like his sisters
shows no interest in weapons.

NEVER DID I THINK WE'D
NOT LOVE EACH OTHER

I remember East Montreal's sky on fire
my sons beaten by their progenitor
the battlefields, the buried mines, black thoughts
to lay to rest.
Because of course
there were happy moments in the life we shared:
the Tunisian beaches
so white
gathering cyclamens
on Mount Boukornine
our walks through the Grunewald
the fruit trees in my parents' garden
dancing on the icy Grand Forks lawn
Christmas celebrations
the joyous life in Montreal
the revolt of students and professors at Loyola
the snow
the slush
and the summer heat
all the meals

fruits
smiles
wine
the boat trips, train trips, car and plane trips
our laughter.
What one calls everyday happiness…
Never did I think we'd not love each other.

ONE DAY

Comes the day when the son becomes a couple.
Beside him
almost all the time
and soon all the time
there's someone
he loves.
Eyes lock.
Misgivings
assessments
kindly
or not
in any case
the mother is no longer often alone with her son.
Nothing is simpler:
he moves out
you need an appointment to see him.
After so many years
there's no more
what I called

affectionately
togetherness.
How strange it is.
She's not unlikeable
besides
this other one
she was bound to appear
and you become acclimatized with no hard feelings
and with the passing of time
to less intimacy
to a plurality
to this other voice on the phone
despite the myths
pitting the daughter-in-law
against the mother…
That's how things happen.
First one son married
then the other.
They're happy
ground rules take hold
distances set in
geographical
emotional
intellectual
distances we don't want to measure.

MY SONS' WIVES

The French word *bru*, or daughter-in-law, comes from the Latin,
and originally meant "young bride."
They're not so young today
my two lovely *brus*
faithfully married for thirty years or more
with these two men
hardy and probably difficult
whom I brought into the world.
It's time I told them that I admire them
these two women
who have
patiently
along with them and their children
built solid families
with no serious quarrels
I admire them
I esteem them
and I thank them.

When you come down to it
have they not
in a sense, at least
granted me my freedom?

CLUMSILY, I HIDE MY DISAPPOINTMENT

In 1971-72, I teach a course called *Women in Modern Society*.
Fifteen three-hour sessions
forty-five women and five men attend a lively debate
between a Jesuit professor of biology, and Henry
Morgentaler...
In 1972 I publish the book *Mother was not a Person*,[11] a
collection of articles by women who had participated in the
course.
Since 1987, the Public Lending Rights Program, every year,
pays me a stipend as compensation for free access to this
book in Canada's public libraries.
How is it then that my sons and daughters-in-law have never
said a single word to me about this book that soon sold six
thousand copies across Canada?
A bad mother turned feminist
one of those who have worked so that women
including her two daughters-in-law, her six granddaughters,
and her four great-granddaughters

---

[11] Content Publishing Limited and Black Rose Books of Montreal.

might have maternity leaves and other rights, including,
one of these days perhaps,
the right to equal pay for equal work?

THE MOTHER WHO WRITES

After this book there were others, twenty or so in all.
"Oh," says Eve, my sister, thinking of our father, our
grandfathers, our uncles, and herself, "everyone in the family
writes."
Perhaps that's the way my sons see their mother:
The one who writes...
That doesn't mean they read her, on paper or on line.
When I was little, I heard every day the click-click-click of
the paternal typewriter.
Why did I wait until the author's death before reading his
painstakingly written novels?
Was the daughter afraid of finding herself, discovering
herself, through her father's eyes?
Does the mother who writes instil fear?
What will she say about me, both one and the other
probably wonder in pondering the question.
They send me a big bouquet of flowers when one of my
books wins a prize... That doesn't mean they've read it.
Let's put her books on one of the shelves
of the glassed-in cabinet, one decides,

and the other will probably follow suit.
It's quickly done,
let's take the time to put them in chronological order.
Unless there's a fire
or one of our children steals one of the volumes,
what she wrote will await
patiently
the moment when we'll be
free enough from her to read her.

FROM SONS TO A DAUGHTER

I'm closer to my daughter than I am to my sons.
Because she's a girl?
We embrace more easily
more often
and without effort.
Is it because she's the only one of the three to talk to me in
German?
It's our secret language.
My sons have lost the language they spoke in Berlin.

Toronto, July 6, 2013. It's a Saturday. I'm writing.
The telephone rings.
"Mama!"
"Yes?"
"It's one o'clock. Have you eaten?"
" … "
"You've forgotten?"
Me, old, forever the object of her attention.

I confess:

"Yes."

I've forgotten. It happens. Even if, according to the seven stages of Dr. Reisberg's scale for Alzheimer's disease, I'm only at Stage 1, that of a healthy adult functioning normally, and this numbering does not imply that such a state is an automatically precarious condition, a necessary prelude to an imminent Stage 2, with the onset of Alzheimer's disease.

She makes us a meal.

"How's your writing going, Marguerite?"

I give a vague reply.

"You said you were going to write two pages about me?"

"Yes, yes."

"You want me to help you?"

I throw myself onto this life preserver.

"Yes!"

She's a lawyer, my daughter, she gives me orally and in writing material that will remind me of her childhood. So it's her childhood she wants me to talk about.

1. You played with me every day.

I don't remember having been such a good mother.

2. When I finished reading a book, you bought me another one. I liked to read. Mainly Doctor Seuss.

You still believed in fiction.

3. One day, in Montreal, there was a man following us. I asked you who it was, and you replied, laughing, that it was my father. He had a habit of walking behind us.

A mystery. He didn't want people really to know him.

4. You taught at Loyola. Often, in the afternoon, you took me to your office, where I waited for you to finish your lecture.
I was eager to see you.

5. In 1970 I got my first identity card from Loyola in Montreal. Look, here it is. I wore a brown T-shirt, with a pretty silk butterfly on the front. You'd bought it for me in Paris.
You were seven years old. You and I, in Paris. Strolling along. Happy.

6. The Loyola office worker asked me to sign the card. I didn't know the meaning of "to sign." So I wrote my name in capital letters, see?
You were always meticulous.

7. On Fridays we went to the faculty club. There was a man there with a python around his neck. You didn't say anything when I touched the big snake.
You weren't delicate. A tough child.

8. At the club, my father never sat at the same table as we did.
I would have liked him to talk to us.

9. In Grand Forks, he took me in his arms at night, when I cried. I don't know where you were…
Bad mother. I was probably at the library.

ALL IS NOT WELL

In our family unit
all is not well.
We are respectable people.
No one runs off at the mouth
there are no rows, no ill feelings
peace reigns.
We talk to each other.
Politics, religion, race, income
are delicate subjects
we touch on
with restraint
and most of the time
not for long.
You might say that we are discreet.
Is that good?
Not entirely, I would say, trying to modulate my voice to
talk here of things we don't want to mention.
Eighty-nine years old, I still hesitate to say out loud, black
on white, that in my family unit not everything is perfect.
It's strange.

I've just acknowledged that I've made mistakes in raising my
three children.
I thought I'd made up for it.
But not all is fine, I repeat.
Perhaps because we're respectable people.
Within our small group
there's a taboo
that in the silence of the family
has slowly become
something unsaid.

THE UNSAID

My daughter was eighteen years old then she announced
that her sexual orientation drew her towards women. My
sons were married, no longer lived with us. Neither she nor I
have talked to them about it.
Myself, I had not anticipated such a revelation: I had
imagined my daughter taking my path, more or less,
completing her studies before marrying an intelligent man
and having children. The idea of seeing her forming a couple
with a woman had never occurred to me, despite my wide
circle of feminist friends, and my zeal for the well-being of
women.
I was concerned for her. I well knew that her style of life
in a society geared towards heterosexuality would be more
difficult than a so-called "normal" one.
I remember having told her that her choice risked subjecting
her to some hostility. She looked at me then, asking me if I
immigrant
divorcee
career woman
writer

atheist
did not find myself
me as well
sometimes
in a certain measure
isolated
sidelined.
My jaw dropped.
At the time, we laughed about it.

THE WALL OF SILENCE

Certainly, time has undone the secret, without our talking
about it.
There's been no harassment
no jokes
or homophobic insinuations
or nervous laughter.
There's been friendship
kindness
on everyone's part
but always this wall of the mute and invisible unsaid.
I ought to have understood that my sons, who each had
three daughters, perhaps feared, without realizing it, that
they could, one or the other, bear the same genes as their
aunt, and thus risk, like her, making the same choice.
Who knows?
"Discreet people do not interfere in the affairs of others,"
says the dictionary.
I have not talked to them about it.
I, discreet, as is proper, as is advisable.
Fear?

Fear what?

Let's be specific.

Or at least try.

Social barriers?

Neighbors who…?

I don't think so.

Professional difficulties?

In our day?

Really!

I could go on analyzing the hidden depths

of this absurd fear

if fear it was

but I'm tired of pondering without finding the right words,

the explanation

me, seedy solipsist[12]

who suspects my sons

who wanted to make war

of having hesitated to say to me

to their sister

to their wives and daughters, what they thought

and I kept silent, me as well.

I should have intervened.

I failed, as a mother, a feminist, and a human being. I kept silent, like them, and she too could have put in her two cents' worth.

I should have spoken about things we didn't want to mention.

When they invited us to dinner

---

[12] In *Murphy*, Beckett describes his protagonist as a "seedy solipsist."

191

me and their sister
why did I not say:
And her friend
her partner
the woman she loves? Is she invited?
It was easier
to say nothing
for fear of making a gaffe perhaps
or causing offence...

ONE WALL OR ANOTHER

Suddenly, the word *wall* gives me a turn:
the familial wall becomes political:
the Berlin wall came down
why not this one?
How?
With the help of what?
In truth, there is nothing available
other than words,
"you must go on…you must say words, as long as there are
any."[13]

---

[13] Samuel Beckett

THERE ARE THE OTHER GENERATIONS

I have six granddaughters and a grandson.
Four great-granddaughters and four great-grandsons.
For the time being. Others may follow, clearly.
And they all talk, talk constantly, talk to each other.
The little ones sometimes talk so fast that you can't grasp
what they're saying.
That delights me.
There are some who make speeches, some who make up
stories, sometimes they all talk at the same time.
I hope they'll never stop.

WRITING OF THE SELF

What?
What did you say?
Writing of the self…
In other words?
It's what?
Very well:
After all, I was a scholar
a professor of French literature
with *Staatsexamen* and doctorate
and later two doctorates honoris causa
so permit me this brief lesson:
The writing of the self
that I prefer
begins in the French literary world
with Montaigne
and there are traces of it in Molière
Pascal gets involved by declaring the self abhorrent
Rousseau puts his definitive stamp on it
it continues with Stendhal and his *The Life of Henry Brulard*
Baudelaire writes *My Heart Laid Bare*

Gide, Proust, Colette, Sartre, Sarraute
each puts in his or her word
one way or another.
In short, the autobiographical text becomes a dominant
twentieth-century genre.
That continues into the twenty-first.
Even if in Quebec the writer is little inclined to confidences
autobiographical writing has made strides
with Gabrielle Roy's *Enchantment and Sorrow* (1984) and others,
including Madeleine Gagnon, who publishes *As Always* in 2013.
In Ontario Mila Younes brings out *Ma mère, ma fille, ma soeur*
Hélène Koscielniak finds her characters through her
encounters and her travels
Pierre Léon intertwines his life, his imagination, and his
immense learning.
And there are others…there will always be others.

A FOOLISH PROJECT?

However the reader clings to his prejudices
against writing often disparaged as being too personal...
Because
and that's the real problem
when faced with a literature of the self
one risks feeling obliged
to protect one's own culture from that of another
one's self versus the account of another self
Well!
Does the reader hope that an impersonal literature will
trouble him less?

IT'S NOT SO EASY,
THIS WRITING OF THE SELF

The Bad Mother
puts on stage
three "I's":
the author
the narrator
and the main character.
Sometimes they merge
sometimes they conspire
sometimes you wonder who's talking.
Three "I's" who co-exist in the same book at different
moments
the past
the present
the future
Really!
Already at school I had problems with my tenses.

BUT WHAT PLEASURE

to discover while writing
memory
that so
gently
step by step
comes
to knock at the door
of the heart
of the brain
of the gut
as the philosopher said
to show the road traveled
the "I" in all its variety
the self
so strange
hateful or not
always eager
to understand
to disclose itself

naked
to see clearly
Mehr Licht, demanded the poet.

acknowledgments

Many thanks to my friends of the North: Johanne Melançon, who encouraged me to practice a less conventional kind of writing, a writing that one might find, perhaps, in an intimate journal; Sylvie Lessard, who, in her role as publicist, always supported me, and above all denise truax, director of Prise de Parole, who believed in *The Bad Mother*, and guided its publication to a wonderfully satisfying conclusion. Finally, my thanks to all those who, while I was writing a text that was for me difficult, tolerated my moods and my silences.

about the author

MARGUERITE ANDERSEN is an accomplished writer and lecturer. She has taught French and translation at several universities and has also worked as a translator and interpreter for diplomats and writers. Andersen was the editor of Canada's first feminist anthology in the 1970s, *Mother was not a person*. She has written several novels, short story collections, and plays.

about the translator

DONALD WINKLER is a Montreal-based literary translator and documentary filmmaker. He has translated Quebec
fiction, non-fiction, and poetry for many years, and is a
three-time winner of the Governor General's Award for
French-to-English translation, most recently, in 2013, for
Pierre Nepveu's collection of verse, *The Major Verbs*.